OPERATION:
Romance

A Welcome to Romance novella

Jessica L. Elliott

Copyright © 2018 Jessica L. Elliott
All rights reserved.
ISBN-10: 1984279181
ISBN-13: 978-1984279187

Dedicated to the quiet romantics and to those who have loved and lost and then loved again.

Oct. 21, 2017

Dear Diary,

Oh. My. Gosh! I think Mom's officially lost it. I mean, I know she's really struggled since Dad left her for that stupid little cheerleader wannabe. Seriously, the girl can't even do a back flip. Lame! But anyway, Mom, just because Dad's a loser going after younger women doesn't mean you need to chase after younger men! Señor Elders is good looking, but he's like half her age! Okay, maybe not half, but still way too young for her and he was at the dance with a really pretty woman. Not sure what the relationship is there. Friend? Girlfriend maybe? Whatever, he's obviously with someone. And today Mom was throwing herself all over him! Ugh! I had to make up a random dance for the teachers just to give him a chance to escape. So embarrassing! Really, I'm glad I saw it before any of my friends did. I hope that kind of behavior hasn't been going on long.

Anyway, I'm obviously going to have to do something about this. I know Mom wants to be in a relationship and I think that would be good for her. She's ready in some ways, but we've got to get her attention redirected. And I've seen how Coach Winston looks at Mom. He'd be perfect for her! He's got to be around the same age, is super friendly, and smart to boot. The guy teaches science classes, after all. Makes you wonder why he's single when he's so good with chemistry. Get it? Okay, bad pun.

The real question is: how am I going to get her to see Coach? He's so quiet. Funny for a guy who spends most of his summer and fall afternoons screaming at football players. But I guess you've got to do something to get their attention. All those hits in the head. Haha. I know he's noticed Mom, I just have to figure out how to get Mom to notice him. I don't think it's going to be easy. But I like a good challenge and I've been reading lots of romances lately, so I know a few tricks.

Okay, I'm going to start making some plans. Get ready for this, world, because Operation: Romance is coming.

Stacie

Chapter 1

Gladys Rosenthal nursed her glass of sparkling cider as her daughter counted down the seconds to New Year's. Single. She was single on New Year's. That hadn't happened since she was fifteen. Worse, her attempts to form any kind of relationship since her divorce had failed miserably. She sighed. Mike had been very patient with her repeated attempts to go out with him. She'd known he wasn't interested and couldn't fathom why she'd kept pushing. Another sigh escaped her lips. Gladys did know what had possessed her. A desperate need to prove she was still attractive and desirable. That had blown up in her face. If she were honest, Gladys would admit the

Spanish teacher probably was a little young for her. No doubt he and his new bride were having a romantic evening together. She took another sip of cider. How had she ended up single on New Year's? Memories of Jesse played through her mind, ending with the day he brought home the cute young thing he'd traded her in for. Anger and hurt swirled against each other in her heart. Hadn't they had good years together? She'd given him everything, supported his every dream. Then he had to go and fall for that ditzy, redheaded…

"Zero!" Stacie shouted and kissed Gladys' cheek. "Happy New Year, Mom."

Gladys attempted to smile and returned her daughter's kiss. "Happy New Year, sweetheart."

Stacie wasn't fooled by her feigned cheerfulness. "I know this past year was awful, but I have a feeling this year is going to be the best one yet."

"What makes you say that?" Gladys asked.

A mischievous twinkle lit Stacie's blue eyes. "Just a feeling." She gave her mother another peck on the cheek. "Well, I'm going to head to bed. Don't stay up too late, okay, Mom?"

Gladys chuckled. "That's supposed to be my

line, dear."

"You know what they say," Stacie retorted with a grin. "Sooner or later your mother will fall out of your mouth."

Laughing, Gladys said, "Oh, get to bed, silly girl."

"Love you, Mom."

"I love you too." Gladys watched her daughter skip up the stairs to her bedroom. Stacie was a junior. How had that happened? All too soon she would be out of the house. Gladys sighed. What would she do without her optimistic daughter around to keep her company?

Pushing those thoughts aside, she walked to the study. It had once been Jesse's home office. Not anymore. After he left, Stacie helped completely redecorate the room. They sold all the furniture and replaced it with new, lighter pieces. Soft blush pink had been painted over the deep blue. In place of Jesse's plaques and certificates of recognition, flower-laden landscapes hung. Gladys sat at one of the matching, whitewashed desks. They had been her favorite find at Good As Old when she'd gone shopping for new furniture. Not only did Adam

Walker give her a bargain price on the set, they were both small enough to fit together in the room without making it claustrophobic. Running a hand over the smooth wood, she allowed herself a wicked grin. Jesse would probably have a heart attack if he saw what they'd done to his "sanctuary." The room was utterly feminine and Gladys loved it.

She picked up a folder on top of her desk. Opening it, she considered what Stacie had said. This year would be the best yet, but probably in ways her daughter wouldn't expect. Other than her volunteer work with the schools, Gladys hadn't worked since Stacie's birth. Being a mother first was always her top priority. But with the divorce finalized, Gladys knew she would need a steady income. One of her dear friends on the PTO board had encouraged her to begin a tutoring business. "It's so needed, especially for some of the students who want to go to college but lack the support at home to learn good study skills."

"How are those students going to be able to afford a tutoring program?"

"Offer them a special discount," her friend replied with a shrug. "There are plenty of parents who can afford to pay a tutor. I've heard some parents are driving to McMinnville and Salem for tutoring. I bet a lot of them would be much happier if there was someone local."

Gladys looked over the paperwork in the folder. She'd been looking at requirements for in-home businesses. It wouldn't be too hard to get set up. And she did have a lot of resources from years of helping Stacie with her homework. The challenge was going to be finding enough clients to make sure she was covering her bills. While Jesse had been faithful in paying child support, she knew it wasn't really enough to cover all their expenses and would end as soon as Stacie turned eighteen. She finished off the glass of sparkling cider and gave herself a resolute nod. Two could play the "I don't need you" game. Gladys was going to prove that she might be older, but that didn't make her less valuable. She jotted some notes in the folder and wrote down a few names of parents she thought might be interested in getting their students a little extra help. School started up again in just three days. By that time, she would have everything ready to start her business. Stacie would be proud of her and she'd be able to make her own mark on the little community of Romance. One that would benefit everyone.

~*~

Stacie finished writing in her diary and glanced at her phone. She couldn't believe how many text messages she'd gotten. Mostly from other girls on the cheer team. She couldn't say she was surprised that only one of her friends from the scholar's bowl team had texted. Most of them had probably gone to bed long before the ringing in of the New Year. But one in particular puzzled her. Johnny Belcarro, the football team captain and most sought after boy in school, had sent her a text. She read it again.

hope u and ur mom have a gr8 new year

Other than an inexplicable warmth flooding her, Stacie wasn't quite sure how to respond to the text. Johnny had never spoken to her. Ever. She wouldn't admit, not even to herself, that she wished he would. Right now the question was, why? Why had he texted her about New Year's? And why had he included her mother in the wish? Unable to come up with a good reason, she decided to simply send a friendly reply. *Thank you. I hope you and your family also have a wonderful New Year!* "Proper spelling and punctuation, dear Johnny. That's the way to a nerdy girl's heart."

thnx

Stacie shook her head and giggled. She stretched with a yawn. Having told her mother not to stay up too late, she should probably take her own advice. There would be time to contemplate Johnny's motives later.

Chapter 2

Stacie walked with her empty lunch tray in hand past the football table. She wasn't sure what it was about the team, but they always sat together and no one else was ever allowed to sit with them. Not even the players' girlfriends, which led to quite a few early breakups for some of them. She allowed herself to sneak a glance at Johnny who was, for lack of a less clichéd word, huddled with the rest of the team. All she could really see was his black-brown hair and broad shoulders. She paused when she heard his voice, low and rich like dark chocolate. "Boy am I glad football season is over. Coach really worked us this year."

"Don't think he's done yet," one of the others groaned. "We've got winter weights now and if we're not up to par, you know what happens next."

"Scholarship lecture," the team said as one.

"What he needs is a wife. Coach Laurence is never so demanding," Johnny said. "But Coach Winston?"

"Hey, he didn't become the winningest coach in Oregon by making things easy," someone else pointed out.

"Winningest at everything but romance," another guffawed.

"Dude, how can you live in Romance and be bad at it?"

"How many breakups have you had this year?"

"Guys, focus," Johnny retorted. "Stacie's mom is single and she's not bad looking, for someone her age. Coach would probably love her."

Stacie's heart quickened. Could she have found an ally for her plot? While she had just started in earnest after New Year's and it had only been a couple weeks, her own attempts to match her mother with Coach Winston had failed. But maybe with help she could get her mom to see what a great guy he really was. She took a micro-step closer.

One of the team members snorted. "Stacie's mom has got it going on."

What good feelings she may have harbored toward the team fled and she marched to the table. She hated that song and couldn't believe the player knew it since the song certainly didn't fit with the rap blasting from his car every day. "My mom hasn't got anything going on, Brady."

Several jumped and one spilled milk down his front. "Dude, football players only," he said angrily.

"As you can see, I'm not sitting at your sacred table," Stacie retorted. "But if you're going to talk about my mom, I'm going to include myself in the conversation. She's gone through enough without you bunch of losers making things harder for her."

"Losers? We never lose."

She started to turn away when she heard a chair knock to the floor and Johnny suddenly had a firm but gentle hold on her arm. "Wait a minute, Rosenthal…"

"Rosenthal?" Stacie repeated, turning to him in disbelief as she pulled her arm from his grip. "I'm not one of your teammates. I've got a first name."

"Stacie, sorry," he said. "Look, we're not making fun of your mom, I promise."

"Not what it sounded like to me," she replied, crossing her arms over her chest. She had to crane her neck to look Johnny in the eyes. Why couldn't she have grown even one more inch in middle school? Trying to stretch her five-foot-nothing frame to look intimidating to a six-foot-plus football player wasn't easy.

"Why don't you have a seat? I have a feeling we can help each other," Johnny added.

"Not a football player," a player whispered.

"What makes you think I need help?" Stacie asked, ignoring the comment, but also refusing the offered chair.

Several of the team members snickered, which Johnny silenced with a glare. Stacie wished she had that kind of influence on people. He turned back to her. "Look, you want your mom to be happy, right?"

"Of course."

"And we want Coach to back off a little. They're both single. Valentine's Day is approaching and with all the hoopla the town will make over it, we should be able to fix them up easy. Your mom gets the nicest guy in town, and Coach gets someone who will distract him just enough to not work us like we're all going out for the NFL. It's a win-win situation."

Stacie narrowed her gaze, trying to determine if Johnny was serious or not. Hard to concentrate when his chocolate-brown eyes pleaded with her to go along with whatever he said. "You're forgetting something. Coach has been single his whole life and my mom just finalized an unpleasant divorce. Just how do you think Mr. Shy-and-Innocent is going to win over a jaded divorcee like my mom?"

Johnny grinned, the left side of his mouth quirking higher than the right. Had the temperature in the cafeteria suddenly spiked? Stacie felt like she was on fire as he said smoothly, "Shawn Winston is the winningest coach in Oregon. With our help, we can give him the best win of his life. Think we can do it, Rosenthal?"

She raised an eyebrow. "Stacie," she corrected. "And you've got yourself a deal. But it's going to take longer than just to Valentine's Day."

"Wanna bet?" Johnny asked with a flirtatious smirk.

"Just what did you have in mind?"

Johnny's grin widened and Stacie could have sworn everyone in the cafeteria could hear the thunderous staccato of her heartbeat. "We get them together by Valentine's Day and you go with me to prom."

Her mouth went dry. She forced herself to ask, "And if you lose this bet?"

"The football team lets the cheerleaders dress us up. Make up, glitter, outfits, whole shebang for the spring assembly."

"Dude, what?"

"No way!"

"Are you nuts?"

Johnny ignored them and leaned down so he was nearly eye-level with Stacie. "What do you say, Rosenthal? Is it a bet?"

She considered his offer. If you wanted to talk about a win-win scenario, he'd just handed it to her on a silver platter. Prom with the hottest guy in school wasn't a loss in her opinion. And the cheer team had been begging to dress the football players up since she was a freshman. The girls would be absolutely thrilled at the prospect. "Not sure you totally understand how a wager is supposed to work,

Johnny," Stacie teased. "Before I agree to anything, we need to determine a couple things. Does 'by Valentine's Day' mean before or are we including it in the countdown?"

"Let's say before."

"Okay, and what exactly do we mean by 'together'? Do they have to just be dating, engaged? I would guess not married."

"Let's call it engaged. That's a lot more official than dating and not as time-consuming as married."

Stacie nodded. "Agreed. All right, you've got a bet."

They shook hands and he smirked. "You can wear any color but pink to prom. I don't do pink."

"That's a shame, Johnny, because I've got a tube of hot-pink lip gloss with your name on it," she retorted.

~*~

Johnny watched Stacie walk away, unable to believe his good fortune. He'd gotten Stacie Rosenthal to agree to go to prom with him. Well, if he won the bet. And that smile when she teased him about the lip gloss? You could melt a glacier with that kind of grin. The protests of his teammates finally broke through his befuddled thoughts and he returned to his seat.

"Dude, what were you thinking?" his best friend asked.

"Come on, Marco, this will be easy. The town is going to do half the work for us anyway," Johnny replied. "All we've got to do is convince Coach to take a chance on love."

"You make it sound like deciding to run a fake or try a throw," Marco retorted.

"Yeah," Brady said. "I don't care what happens, you're not putting me in a dress. Not in front of the whole school."

"Then you guys better help me out so we win the bet."

"What are we getting out of this?"

"Not having to dress up like a girl?" Johnny offered.

"You're going to have to do better than that, pal," Marco pointed out.

"Pizza and video game night on me?"

The team cheered. "That's more like it," Brady shouted. "So, what's the plan?"

"First things first, we find a way to hint that

Coach should ask her out."

"Do they even know each other?" Marco asked. "This will never work if they don't."

"Oh yes," Johnny replied. "I've seen the two of them at school activities. I think he's been trying to work up the nerve to say something but hasn't yet. Time for a team pep talk."

Their kicker, Tyler, said, "That's all well and good, but how are you going to get him to talk to her?"

"Tell him to give Stacie's mom some ideas of potential clients. She just started a tutoring business."

"How do you know that, Garrett?" Marco asked.

The teen's ears turned pink. He mumbled something indistinguishable, but Johnny guessed at what he was saying. It wouldn't surprise him if Garrett was getting tutoring. The poor guy struggled in several of his classes.

"Doesn't matter," Johnny said, sparing Garrett further embarrassment. "That gives us an opening. Coach is a science teacher and would definitely know of some students Mrs. Rosenthal could help."

Brady rubbed his hands together. "This is gonna be good."

"Better hope so," Marco muttered. "Or we're going to be humiliated at the spring assembly."

Chapter 3

Shawn Winston gathered up stacks of homework to grade. He saw one of his football players enter the classroom. "Hello, Johnny. Ready for winter weights?"

The teen grinned. "Aren't I always ready?"

Shawn laughed. "Seems that way. I'm going to head that way myself once I take these papers to my car. What can I do for you?"

"You know Stacie Rosenthal, yeah?"

"Sure, she's in my honors chemistry class. Why?" Shawn asked. He gave a teasing wink. "You thinking of asking her out? If so, I heartily approve, as long as you keep your focus where it needs to be."

"No! Well, I mean, yeah, I'd like to, but no, that wasn't my point," Johnny stammered, his face going as red as his letter jacket.

Shawn laughed. "I'm teasing you, Belcarro. If you're not asking for dating advice, why did you bring up Stacie?"

"Did you know her mom is starting a tutoring business?"

Shawn raised an eyebrow. "No, I didn't know that." He glanced at Johnny. "I don't think you need tutoring, though. You've got really good grades."

"Oh, I wasn't thinking of it for me. I just thought maybe you could talk to Mrs. Rosenthal about potential clients. I'm sure you know of some students who could use a little help."

Frowning, Shawn replied, "That's a nice thought and I'd like to help her. But privacy laws being what they are, I can't discuss with her which students are struggling and which aren't."

"So you don't tell her directly." Johnny shrugged. "Talk to the parents at conferences. Or if you've got students who are struggling, suggest they talk to her. Maybe you could see if she's got cards or whatever that you could pass out to people. I bet if you asked her how you could help, she'd have some great ideas."

"That's possible," Shawn admitted, walking out of the classroom. "I'll have to think about it. For now, though, you need to get to winter weights. I'll be there in a bit." As Johnny disappeared down a hallway, Shawn moved toward the parking lot. He wasn't sure what had prompted the junior to talk to him about Mrs. Rosenthal's new venture, but it did give him a way to strike up a conversation with her. Possibly. He hadn't seen the PTO president recently. Of course, being that he was at winter weights every afternoon, he probably missed seeing her when she arrived for meetings.

He sighed as he reached his car. Too busy. That's what his mother always told him. "You're too busy to pursue a relationship," echoed in his mind as he set the stacks in the vehicle. But what else was he supposed to do? Shawn had worked hard to build a reputation as a coach of winning football teams. That meant daily practices, summer camps, winter weights, meeting with the middle school coaches and watching their players, and then of course the actual games. Coaching was time-consuming, but he loved every minute of it. Watching his boys pull together and become a unit made all the extra work worthwhile. And while none of his players had ever gone on to play for the NFL, there were several playing for big schools, including the University of Oregon and Oregon State. And those who had moved on from college were successful in the careers they'd chosen. That brought him all the joy and pride a parent could feel for a child. At least, he figured it was as close as he was likely to get. With his next birthday bringing him to thirty-nine, it was unlikely he'd ever have a wife, let alone children to feel proud of. So he adopted his boys, each of the players on each football team. In that way he had more children than would ever have been possible any other way.

But he knew it wasn't just busyness that kept him single. For a man who could easily command the attention of high school boys, gaining the attention of an attractive female was disappointingly challenging. Though he occasionally had thoughts he would classify as romantic, verbalizing those thoughts didn't come easily. The few times he'd attempted had never ended well. What was it about women that made them so difficult to understand?

"Hey, watch it!" a voice snapped as he ran headlong into someone.

Shawn looked up from the pavement and was horrified to see Gladys Rosenthal glowering up at him. Diminutive like her daughter, she resembled a pixie with her short blonde hair and sparkling blue eyes. At the moment, an angry pixie. "I'm so sorry."

"Coach, I realize you're used to tackling people," Gladys retorted, "but you might at least save it for people who are big enough to return the favor."

It was all he could do not to laugh aloud. *Tackling? If I tackled her, she'd know it and likely wouldn't get up for a week.* However, he didn't want to raise the woman's ire. "I am sorry, Mrs. Rosenthal. I wasn't watching where I was going, and clearly I should have been."

Her expression softened somewhat. "No harm done. Where were you going in such a hurry?"

"Winter weights," he remembered, "and I'm late."

"Don't let me keep you then," she said. "Have a good day, Coach Winston."

I wouldn't mind being kept by you, Shawn thought. "Yeah, um, you too," he stammered before turning toward the building. He had taken three steps when he turned. "I heard you're starting a tutoring business."

Gladys sighed. "I'm trying to. The kids who really need it can't afford it and those who can don't want it."

His heart went out to her. He knew she'd recently divorced and imagined her budget must be feeling the pinch of that lost income. Of course, her feelings were probably a bit trampled too. Shawn couldn't imagine what would possess a man to leave her. If he ever managed to find a woman like Gladys Rosenthal, he'd hold on and never let go. "Perhaps I could help you out."

She studied him. "How?"

Yeah, Coach, how? a voice nagged. "Well, if you've got a business card or something, I could give those out to students I think could benefit from tutoring. I could even volunteer to help out with some of the tutoring, just as a volunteer. You wouldn't have to pay me or anything."

Gladys considered for a moment. "I'll have to think about it and check what the rules on that sort of thing are. I'd hate to have the IRS jumping down my throat because I wasn't paying someone who ought to be paid. Besides, wouldn't you be too busy to help tutor?"

"I guess you're right," Shawn replied, cursing his rigorous schedule for the first time. "It was just a thought." *Don't screw this up! Say something else*, the nagging voice shouted. "Just let me know if there's ever anything I can do to help you out. I know things must be hard right now."

She quirked an eyebrow. "Oh?"

"With the divorce and everything." *I am an idiot*, he thought as Gladys frowned. "I mean, I figure that would be tough, right?" Frustrated that his lame attempts at conversation were making the situation worse, Shawn finished, "If you need anything, just tell me."

"Yeah, thanks."

As he watched her walk away he muttered, "Way to blow it, Winston." His mood thoroughly soured, he strode back to the high school to begin the weight training session. Filled with student athletes and a few students who just wanted to work out, the after school program allowed him an extra chance to work with his team. It wasn't a requirement, but most of his starting players participated. Within twenty minutes, most of them looked like they'd rather be anywhere but the weights room. A few glared at him openly. Shawn didn't care though. If he were to tell them the truth, he had no interest in being there that day either. He would much prefer to be with Mrs. Rosenthal, trying to find a way to convince her to forgive him for being a moron.

Chapter 4

After finishing her tutoring session with Garrett Baker, Gladys drove to Finding Forever Animal Rescue, trying to put Coach Winston out of her mind. Why on earth would he bring up her divorce? Like she really needed anyone reminding her that her love life had fallen apart in the worst possible way. She rolled her eyes. The man was pretty dense, despite those dreamy blue eyes. Gladys shook her head. Dreamy? No, that word no longer existed in her vocabulary. Men were nothing but trouble and she was done with them. Especially any who might make the word dreamy creep into her mind. Shawn Winston was nothing more than her daughter's chemistry teacher. While he may be handsome with eyes like forget-me-nots and thick dark hair most men his age wished they had, Gladys had no intentions of fumbling with her heart again. This time she planned to keep it safely tucked away and her defensive line at the ready.

She cleared her thoughts as she pulled into the animal shelter's parking lot. Stacie may have thought she was subtle, but that girl was as easy to read as a billboard. She knew Stacie was trying to get her set up with the coach. But Gladys was determined not to let that happen. No hint that she'd been thinking of Shawn Winston would show and therefore no encouragement to Stacie. Gladys parked the car and walked inside the old farmhouse. The volunteer at the help desk smiled. "Hello, Gladys. Stacie's back with the dogs."

Gladys stifled a grimace. "Of course she is. Thanks, Sally." She walked to the room with kennels, a sigh escaping her. She knew how badly Stacie wanted a dog. Always had. But Jesse's allergies made it impossible. *Jesse no longer lives with you*, a voice in her head reasoned. Her heart nearly stopped when she saw her daughter cradling a tiny pup in her arms, feeding it with some kind of bottle.

Stacie hadn't yet realized that she'd entered the room, her entire focus centered on the puppy she nursed. Calm, quiet words flowed from her as she rocked the little animal. She looked up with a radiant smile when Gladys cleared her throat. "Oh my gosh, Mom, have you ever seen anything so precious?"

She glanced down at the puppy. Scrawny was the first word that came to mind with motley as a close second. Half of the puppy's fur appeared to have been rubbed out, though she couldn't imagine how. Little ribs showed under the skin and it was clear the poor thing hadn't been able to eat properly before being picked up. Gladys couldn't even begin to imagine what kind of dog the little runt would grow into. "What is it?"

"She's a puppy," Stacie giggled.

Gladys smirked at her. "I know it's a puppy. What kind?"

"Dr. Foster says it'll be a few weeks before we know."

"I thought the Fosters were only here on Fridays," Gladys said.

"Normally they are. But Brent said he would

take care of the puppy during the day and night since she requires a lot of attention. Since Tuesday and Wednesday are my volunteer days and I want to be a veterinarian, Amanda agreed to come on Tuesdays too to check on the pup and teach me how to take care of an abandoned pup. She's sent for a DNA test with a cheek swab so we can find out what kind of puppy Frenchy is." Stacie snuggled the puppy. "She's so adorable."

"She's a homely little thing, don't you think?" Gladys asked, hoping beyond hope Stacie wouldn't ask the same question she asked every time she met a new dog at the shelter.

Stacie rolled her eyes. "You would be too if you'd been living under a bush for Lord only knows how long. We're lucky she's even still alive. Without her mother and with all the cold we've had it's a miracle she didn't freeze to death." She kissed the puppy's forehead. Then she turned pleading eyes to her mother. "Oh, Mom, don't you think I could take her home? I would take wonderful care of her and Dad won't be there, so his allergies don't matter anyway. And because she's a puppy, we can raise her and train her right from the beginning. So a lot of behavior problems can be avoided. Please?"

Gladys couldn't argue any of Stacie's points. "What about when you go to school?"

"Come on, that's the lamest excuse ever. Lots of kids have pets."

"I'm not talking about high school," Gladys chided. "You graduate next year. What will you do with her then?"

Stacie shrugged. "Take her with me? I'd find a way to make it work."

"And your school-work now?"

"I've been spending every spare moment I could at the shelter for months now and my grades have never dipped."

Gladys sighed. "I'll have to think about it."

"Good," Dr. Allie Foster said as she entered the room, "because this little one won't be ready to leave for a few weeks yet. We've got to get her healthy before anyone takes her home."

"I could do that," Stacie insisted as the veterinarian gently took the puppy and bottle from her. "I could help her become strong and healthy."

"I'm afraid your mom does have a good point, Stacie. This poor girl is going to need a lot of care.

Care you won't be able to give while you're at school. For now, Brent's going to do most of the care and have volunteers help when they can. Once she's in the clear and we know her genetic make-up, I'm sure she'd be ready for adoption."

Stacie looked at her mother. "Please, Mom?" she begged.

Gladys shook her head with a slight smile. "We'll see, okay? In the meantime, you may as well get her used to you."

Stacie threw her arms around her mother before turning to the creamish puppy Dr. Foster held. "Hear that, Frenchy? That's Mom's way of saying yes without admitting it."

"Why Frenchy?" Gladys asked.

"Because of all the Pink Ladies, Frenchy is my favorite. Plus Rizzo would be a weird name for such a sweetheart."

Allie laughed. "I'll let Brent know this baby girl has a name and a potential home. But, Stacie, I am serious. It's going to be quite a few weeks before she can go home with you. Abandoned pups need a lot of constant care and until I know what kind of dog she is, I can't be sure she's growing properly."

Stacie sighed. "I understand." She leaned over to kiss the puppy's head one more time before turning to her mother. "All right. I guess now I'm ready to go home and work on my homework."

Gladys chuckled. "Will you survive without your new baby?"

The teen whipped out her phone and swiped the screen. "I'll never be without Frenchy again," she replied, showing off a picture she'd snapped earlier.

As Stacie walked out of the room, Gladys leaned over to Allie. "Thank you for that. I'm not sure I could have convinced her to leave the dog here!"

"Don't thank me yet. Frenchy's not going to be some dainty little thing. There's no way for me to tell you if that means she'll be German shepherd large or a giant. My instincts tell me she's not going to be small. Better start getting your house ready. You would break Stacie's heart if you told her no."

Gladys nodded and left the room. Stacie chattered the entire way home about her new puppy. She listened for a while before sighing, "Listen, sweetie, I really meant it when I said we'll see."

"But, Mom, she's so perfect and little."

"She is now, but babies grow up. Frenchy may

be a runty thing today, but who knows how big she'll get? Dr. Foster seems to think she could get quite large."

"So?"

Gladys gave Stacie her best mom glare. "So nothing, young lady. If you want to keep Frenchy, you're going to have to prove that you're ready, and I'm not talking about responsibility. I know you're responsible enough for a dog. But you'll need to dog proof the house and start gathering supplies. You need to read up on puppy care and training. You need to decide what rules the dog has to follow. You have to show you're prepared to have a pet; mentally, physically, and financially. Otherwise, Frenchy stays at Finding Forever."

"Okay, deal," Stacie said with a grin. "Don't worry, Mom, Frenchy will be the best behaved dog you've ever seen!"

"To go along with my perfect daughter." Gladys smiled.

They arrived home and each went to their desk in the study. Stacie put in earbuds and plopped her school books on the desk. After watching her daughter for a few moments to confirm she was staying on task, Gladys sent a few emails and made some notes in her planner. She then glanced over her budget. If Stacie was bringing home a dog, she needed to work that into the monthly expenses. *Please let Frenchy stay small*, she prayed before spending the remainder of the early evening getting things set up for her business venture. She'd gotten a few parents interested in it, and the school counselors promised to keep her name on hand to give out when appropriate. Coach Winston had also mentioned giving her information out to students he thought could use it. Business cards was what he'd said. Probably a good idea to get some made. In fact, it was a wonderful idea.

Gladys jotted down a few more notes before heading to the kitchen to make some dinner. She sighed as she thought about everything she was trying to do. Her mother always used the quote about a journey starting with a single step. This felt more like a giant leap of faith. But if things worked out well, she'd be able to support herself and Stacie through whatever might come up in their future. That in and of itself was worth a little uncertainty.

Chapter 5

Though he knew he needed to go to sleep, Shawn remained at his desk attempting to grade papers. He took off his reading glasses and raked a hand through his hair. He couldn't get the botched conversation with Gladys Rosenthal out of his mind. The way she'd glared at him was worse than when he'd bumped into her. "How am I going to fix this?" he wondered aloud. He picked up a nearby newspaper. An ad for Romantic Blooms caught his eye. "Twenty percent off any large bouquet? Hmmm." A million thoughts flew through his mind. What if she didn't like the flowers he sent? Or what if she was allergic to them? If he picked the same kind her ex-husband used to send, would she be offended? Had he even ever sent her flowers?

Quit being a coward, Coach, and cut the coupon out, the nagging voice insisted. He refused to examine why that voice sounded a lot like his mother's. Instead, he grabbed a pair of scissors and carefully cut around the coupon. He could go to the flower shop during his planning period and have something delivered. It could be a pleasant surprise for her. He turned his attention back to the stack of papers and finished grading before walking to his bedroom for the night. Surely a gesture of goodwill would win him some points with Mrs. Rosenthal.

~*~

Shawn parked in front of Romantic Blooms and sat in his car staring at the door for a good three minutes before finally deciding to go through with his plan. The owner, Cheryl Montgomery, glanced up as he walked in. "Oh, hello, Coach Winston. Haven't seen you in here for a long time."

"Probably better that way," he replied, remembering the last time he'd come to the store. One of his players had been killed in a car accident and he'd come to Romantic Blooms to get flowers for the teen's parents.

"Well, hopefully you're here for a happier reason," Cheryl said.

He shrugged. "I think that will depend on how the flowers are received."

"Get yourself in trouble with one of the moms?" she teased.

"Sort of," Shawn said slowly, unwilling to go into too many details. Romance wasn't an itty-bitty town, but it was small enough that he didn't want rumors starting. "Anyway, what sort of bouquet would you recommend as an apology?"

Cheryl laughed. "Oh, I suppose that depends on how badly you messed up, Coach. If it was a minor infraction, probably this bouquet over here would work well," she said, motioning to a small arrangement of daisies and yellow roses. "But if you really stuck your foot in it, you're going to want something more along the lines of this." She picked up a blue vase filled with roses, lilies, and flowers Shawn couldn't even name in a variety of shades from white to blue. "Of course, if you want it to also be romantic, I could do the same sort of arrangement with purple or red," she added.

"How bad is bringing up a sensitive topic?"

She pushed the bouquet closer to him. "I suggest you go all out, Coach Winston. The only way to win at the game of love is to run your best plays."

He felt heat crawl up his neck. "Who says love is involved?"

Winking, Cheryl said, "You can't fool a florist. Now, do you want this arrangement or a similar one in a different color?"

He looked at the flowers. They were perfect for January and made him think of snow and frost. But did he really want Gladys to remain frosty? No. Definitely not. "Can you do something similar with red and pink?"

"Of course I can. Here," she said, handing him a card and envelope. "Write a heartfelt message to go with your flowers and then do you want to deliver them yourself? Or shall I deliver them for you?"

"Well," Shawn began. He wasn't sure he wanted to see Gladys' reaction. Then again, maybe he was just finding the easy way out again. It wouldn't hurt too much to deliver them himself. Unless, of course, Gladys chased him off and yelled at him for being an insensitive cad. That would hurt. "Yeah, why don't you deliver them? I think it would be better that way."

"Sure thing. Just tell me the address and I'll be sure they arrive for the lucky lady."

Shawn finished his purchase before going back out to his car. "Wimp," he muttered as he drove to the high school.

~*~

Gladys frowned as the doorbell interrupted her work. She was tempted to ignore it until the unbidden intruder went away but couldn't bring herself to act on the temptation. She sighed as she walked to the door. Surprise replaced annoyance when she opened the door to see the local florist standing with a large, beautiful bouquet. "What's this?"

"Flowers, of course. I hope you'll forgive Coach Winston for whatever he did," Cheryl replied as she handed Gladys the vase. "I haven't seen him look that nervous since we almost lost the qualifying game for state. Have a great day!"

"Forgive him? For what?" Gladys murmured as she closed the front door. Perhaps there had been a mistake. She looked at the card. It took her a minute to decipher her name out of the chicken scratch

Shawn Winston called handwriting. She set the vase on her dining table. Pink lilies and roses, red carnations, pure white daisies and baby's breath, as well as other fragrant blooms brought needed light and color to the room. She smiled despite herself. Gladys sat down and opened the card.

Gladys, I'm really sorry about the awkward conversation yesterday. My people skills are sometimes lacking. I wish you great success in your tutoring venture and if there's anything I can do to help, let me know. I'll make time for you.

The next sentences were written so hastily Gladys had to spend several moments examining them before she made any sense of the missive.

I'd really like to spend more time with you. If you're interested, meet me at Della's Diner at noon on Saturday. ~~*Coach*~~ *Shawn Winston*

She shook her head at the crossed-out title. Shawn was no doubt used to signing things as a coach. But the sentences before the signature puzzled her. Had he really just asked her out using a bouquet of flowers? She supposed it was better than a text message, certainly more beautiful, but really? A smile quirked her lips. Saturday was pretty open and it would be nice to give the coach a chance to redeem himself, though the flowers were certainly a nice start. She breathed in the soft fragrance, then pulled out her phone and added *Lunch with S. Winston* to her calendar. A glance at the time told her it was time to pick Stacie up and drop her off at the animal shelter. As much as she enjoyed every moment with her daughter, she looked forward to finding an old junker for the teen to drive. Something that would be reliable in Oregon's winter weather while at the same time not being anything fancy. She remembered the girl in her graduating class who'd been given a brand-new Mustang for her birthday only to crash and total it within a week. Why her parents had then gotten her a second sports car eluded Gladys. Her parents hadn't given her a car at all.

When she arrived at the high school, Stacie stood outside the building, talking to a tall, muscular young man. Football player, if build and letter jacket were any indication. Curiosity bubbled within her as Stacie nodded and waved to him while skipping to the car. Gladys caught the words, "See you then, Rosenthal."

"Bye!" Stacie called as she got in the car.

"Who was that, dear?" Gladys asked. She fought

a smile from her face as Stacie's face went crimson and she fumbled with her seatbelt.

"Just a friend," Stacie hedged.

"You don't blush for just friends," Gladys pointed out with a smirk. "What's his name?"

"Johnny."

Gladys raised an eyebrow. "Johnny? As in Johnny Belcarro?"

"Yes."

"How did you end up on his radar?"

Stacie glared at her. "It's not like I'm hideously ugly, Mom."

Gladys frowned. "That's not what I meant, sweetheart, and you know it. Johnny is incredibly popular and you've never mentioned him before."

"I didn't know I had to give you a play-by-play of my life."

"Anastasia Lorraine, that was uncalled for."

"So was your question." The ride continued in uncomfortable silence. Stacie unbuckled her seatbelt as they stopped in the parking lot of Finding Forever. "Johnny and I have been in classes together off and on since middle school," she said, turning to face her mother. "I don't talk about him because until recently we never talked to each other. I'll see you at five thirty."

Gladys watched Stacie stomp toward the farmhouse. She sighed, hating to admit her daughter was right. Her question had been badly worded. But she desperately needed to know how close Stacie was to the football star. She knew something about football players, having been married to one. The last thing she wanted was to see her daughter get hurt.

Chapter 6

Stacie cuddled Frenchy close while giving the pup her afternoon bottle. "Can you believe she said that?" she asked. "I mean, really. How did I get on Johnny's radar? I'm not exactly repulsive, am I? And what does that even mean? I don't think I've ever heard anyone say that before."

The pup hiccupped.

"You're right," she sighed. "It's not worth worrying about." Her cell phone dinged and she pulled it out.

time sat?

Stacie rolled her eyes. She sent back, *Is there a question in there?* Though she already knew what

Johnny meant, she was determined to see him write out proper sentences in their communication.

What time should we meet on Saturday? Better, Miss Grammar?

Much. Stacie thought for a moment. When her mother added the lunch date to her schedule, she'd obviously forgotten that she and Stacie had their calendars synced so that they didn't run into scheduling conflicts. The time for that was set for noon. However, there was no location and nothing indicated whether or not the coach would be picking her up. If she and Johnny were going to go on a reconnaissance mission, as he'd called it, they would need to be able to follow the couple. *Maybe pick me up at 11:45.*

She snuggled the pup again as it whimpered. "There, there, Frenchy. I'm not ignoring you. Here, let's take a picture together." She held the puppy up close to her face with one hand and took a selfie with the other. The message icon flashed.

k

"Seriously, Johnny?" Stacie put the phone away just as Dr. Foster walked in.

"How's our littlest patient doing?"

Stacie smiled. "Just finished her bottle. But I thought you were only going to come on Tuesdays?"

"Normally I will, but I realized with everything going on yesterday, we forgot to take her measurements. Since it's been a slow day at the clinic, I thought I'd come in and see how Frenchy is doing. Let's weigh and measure her so we can track her growth."

"How old do you think she is?" Stacie asked.

"We're going to try to determine that today. Has she eliminated on her own at all?"

"No, she only goes when I use the cotton ball."

Allie made a note on her chart. "Okay. While not fun for us, it does help us figure out how old she is. Bring her over here to the scale." She took note of the puppy's length and weight. Then she checked her vital signs. "The good news is her ears are open. So she is hearing all that chattering you do."

"Hey!"

She winked. "It's good to talk to her; she needs to know she isn't alone. Her eyes haven't opened yet, so this poor baby can't be more than two weeks old." Cuddling the pup, Allie murmured, "How did you survive, little one?"

"If she's that young, she couldn't have been alone long," Stacie said. "She would have died."

"Yes, that's true."

"Is it possible her mother is out there and the person who rescued her just missed seeing her? What if there are other puppies? What if the mother is sick? Or hurt?"

"Calm down, Stacie," Allie said gently. "I'll send someone out to scan the area. It is possible the rescuer missed seeing the rest of this girl's family. It's also possible that she was abandoned for whatever reason and we just happened to have someone in the right place at the right time."

Stacie frowned. She couldn't stand the idea that someone would just abandon the puppy.

"Why don't you go walk some of the other dogs? I'll make some more notes about Frenchy and then I'll go search the area myself."

"Can I go with you?"

"Not today, Stacie. Brent needs all the help he can get around here. And," she sighed, "if she was abandoned with a litter, what I find may not be pleasant. Stay here and walk the dogs. That will be a much happier task." Allie smiled. "If I hurry, you might still be here when I get back."

"I guess I'll try to be patient."

~*~

Gladys walked into the shelter just as Allie Foster arrived carrying a towel in one hand and holding the leash of a giant, filthy dog in the other. "What is that?"

"She's a Great Pyrenees and if I'm correct, she's the mother of Stacie's Frenchy."

Heart sinking, Gladys asked, "Are you sure?"

"We'll find out in a moment."

Stacie looked up as they walked into the room. "I walked all the dogs and heard Frenchy whimpering," she began as the adults entered. Her eyes widened as she took in the large dog Allie led. "Is that Frenchy's mother?"

The dog let out a loud bark and reached for the puppy in Stacie's hands.

"I would say so. Why don't we see if Frenchy can nurse while I try to get her brother and sister cleaned up?"

"She has a brother and sister?" Stacie squealed. "Oh! Let me see!" Allie gently held out the tiny puppies she'd wrapped in the towel. "They're so cute! Poor babies look half-starved though."

"Just like Frenchy. Based on the mother's condition, I think the litter was abandoned. She must have run away from home to find her babies. It's a shame only these three survived."

"How do you know?"

Allie shook her head. "Let's not go into detail. Anyway, Great Pyrenees typically have at least six puppies. Sometimes fewer, but this is a breed known for large litters. Go get the largest crate we have. I'll have to bring a whelping box from home since Brent doesn't usually have any on hand. But for now, a large crate will work."

Stacie went to do as she was told while Allie reintroduced Frenchy to her mother. "I'm sorry, Gladys," Allie said after a moment. "I did warn you Frenchy could be large."

"Yes, you did. That's not what concerns me."

"Why are you frowning then?"

Gladys looked the veterinarian in the eye. "How am I going to convince Stacie to just bring one puppy home? She's fallen in love with the whole litter and the mama to boot. I can tell."

Allie chuckled. "Sorry, Gladys, you're on your

own there."

"On her own for what?" Stacie asked.

"Nothing you need to worry about," Gladys said firmly. "Do you need anything else?" she directed to Allie.

"Well, if you guys can keep the puppies warm, this poor mama needs a bath."

"Oh, of course we can! Mom, you hold Frenchy. I'll hold Zuko and Marty."

Gladys took the puppy from Stacie. She had to admit, Frenchy was starting to look a little cute. She wrapped the warm towel a bit tighter around the pup as it shivered.

"She's growing on you, isn't she?" Stacie said with a smile.

"Maybe," Gladys replied slowly.

"You know, Mom, we've got a really big yard…"

"No, Stacie, one new dog would be a huge undertaking. But four?"

"Oh, come on, Mom," Stacie pleaded. "We could do it. And once Cha-Cha is feeling better, we could take her and the puppies home."

"How do you name them so fast?" Gladys asked.

Stacie smirked. "They tell me their names when I see them. It wasn't that hard to name me, was it? Anyway, they would be great companions for us. And you could keep at least one of them when I go to college and you won't feel so lonely without me. Cha-Cha would be perfect; she's a great mom, just like you."

"Flattery will get you nowhere, Stacie," Gladys said, though she smiled. "Shouldn't we find out if the mama already has an owner?"

"What? You wouldn't really let them take her back, would you?"

"After finding the abandoned pups, most likely not," Allie said. "But knowing who owned her could help us find out why the pups were abandoned to begin with. I doubt at their age it was accidental, but it is possible."

"Would that mean, I couldn't keep any of the puppies?" Stacie asked, a frown settling over her features.

Allie nodded. "If it was truly an accident, yes. They would need to be returned to their rightful owner. However, they're awfully young to have been on any kind of outing, especially in this weather. I don't think you have anything to worry about." She finished toweling down the large dog's fur. "Now, let's put Cha-Cha and her puppies in the crate and let them all get reacquainted. Thanks for your help, Stacie. I'll see you on Tuesday. Hopefully then I'll have some answers for you both."

Gladys and Stacie helped get the family in the crate. Gladys watched her daughter take several photos with her phone and then looked at the dog Stacie had dubbed Cha-Cha. The large white dog cuddled and licked her puppies with an expression that could only be defined as adoration. She'd felt the same way when Stacie was born. She couldn't imagine what the dog had gone through to find her lost pups. Gladys glanced once more at Stacie. Perhaps they could make room in their home for a family of dogs who needed a fresh start.

Chapter 7

Saturday morning, Shawn woke up early. He put on running shorts, a T-shirt, and his running shoes before walking outside. The cold January air bit his exposed skin, but he ignored it. He'd warm up soon enough. His neighbors probably all thought he was crazy to be running at this time of year, particularly with so little to protect him from the elements. For Christmas, one neighbor had gotten him several pairs of running tights and his football players had brought him at least a dozen long-sleeved shirts. They'd be good for days with a lot of snow or wind, but for now he felt fine without.

His thoughts wandered to his potential date that

afternoon as he ran briskly through the streets of his neighborhood. If he'd been smart, Shawn knew he would have left a phone number for Gladys to reach him at. But he justified not having it by telling himself that surprises were romantic. Maybe she'd show up and maybe she wouldn't. At the time, it had seemed like a great idea. Now he really wished he knew whether or not he'd be eating by himself.

As he arrived back at his house, he slowed his pace. He stretched for a few minutes once in the warmth of his home. It was a small house, a starter home really, but he'd been calling it home for the last ten years. Walls decorated with football posters from the high school and a few from his college years and simple furniture rounded out the rooms. He wandered to the bathroom to shower and shave. Just as he was finishing, his phone rang. Wrapping a towel around his middle quickly, he moved into the bedroom where his phone was. He glanced at the caller ID and grimaced. "Good morning, Mom."

"Good morning, Shawn, dear. How are you today?"

"I'm fine, Mom. You're up early."

"Not that early, dear. It's nearly eight o'clock. I

assume you've gone on your run already."

"Yep, I just got out of the shower."

"You're decent, aren't you?"

Shawn debated about answering truthfully. "I'm covered."

"Good. Because I'll be at your house in precisely one minute."

"Wait, what?" The line went dead and Shawn bit back a curse. Hurriedly getting dressed, he ran out to the living room just as his mother knocked on the door. "What a surprise, Mom. I didn't expect you to visit."

"The idea of spending Valentine's Day alone didn't appeal to me," she replied, following him into the house. "Since you seem accustomed to it, I thought I'd see how you manage it."

"Ouch, Mom. Love you too," he said.

She gave his arm a playful smack. "Really, Shawn, a handsome man like you has no business staying single forever."

"So if I were ugly, it wouldn't matter?"

"Don't put words in my mouth, son." Miranda Winston gave her son a long look. "You're dressed awfully nice for a Saturday. Did I interrupt your plans?"

"Well…"

"What's her name?"

"Pardon?"

"Don't play simple with me, Shawn Winston. What is the lady's name?"

Shawn ran a hand through his hair. While he had his father's broad build, his dark hair and sapphire-blue eyes were inherited from his mother. Right now her blue eyes were boring a hole in his forehead. "What if I told you I was meeting with some of the other coaches?"

Miranda scoffed. "I would remind you that you don't wear cologne to a meeting with the coaches. I'm not giving up here. Tell me who she is or I'll simply follow you, wherever you're going, and introduce myself."

"Good grief, Mom, that's a little over the top, don't you think?"

"Name."

He sighed. "I'm meeting Gladys Rosenthal for lunch. Since you've never lived here in Romance, that name won't mean anything to you."

"Gladys, a nice name. And is she pretty?"

"Sure."

Miranda gave him another once-over. "I suggest you put shoes on before going on this lunch date."

Shawn rolled his eyes. "I didn't plan to go barefoot. You caught me off guard."

"I assume you merely had a towel around your nether regions when I called?"

Shaking his head, he admitted, "Something like that."

"Well, I'm famished. Let's have some breakfast and you can tell me all about Gladys and how long you've been courting her."

Shawn hid a grimace as he led her to the kitchen. "So, how long did you say you were staying?" he asked as he whisked together pancake batter.

"Oh, at least until Valentine's Day. I would have gone to Judy's, but I wouldn't want to spoil her plans with Roger." Miranda sat down at the tiny excuse of a table Shawn owned.

"You wouldn't have been spoiling it. I'm sure they'd both appreciate having someone available to watch the girls for them."

"Precisely why I didn't want to go. Judy would either cancel her plans to keep me company or leave me at the mercy of the twins. I'm not sure which would be worse."

Shawn chuckled. "Now, Mom, you love May and Rose. And if pictures are anything to go off, Suzie and Maisie look to be about the cutest things God ever created."

"Well, yes, they are rather precious," Miranda said with a smile. "Though I don't know how Judy stays sane. Two sets of twins just two years apart? I'm sure I would have died."

"You managed one set of twins rather well."

"One set, yes, but all the rest of my children came one at a time and I much preferred it that way." She eyed him suspiciously. "And you are getting me off-topic. Tell me about this woman you're meeting."

Cursing his bad luck, Shawn said, "What's to tell? She volunteers with the PTO and I'm meeting her for lunch today. Her daughter is in my honors chemistry class."

"I might just get a grandchild out of you yet!" Miranda teased with a smile.

"Don't marry me off just yet. We haven't been dating at all. This is the first, and maybe only, date."

"Oh, what a terrible attitude," Miranda scoffed.

"Of course this will lead to more dates. And a wedding too, if I can wrangle one."

"Mom, please don't start plotting anything. Remember what happened with Tara?"

Miranda rolled her eyes. "How can I not? You bring her up every time I mention dating. Well, if you don't want my help, I won't interfere. Once we finish our meal, I'll just see myself to your guest room and you can enjoy your lunch date. I'm rather tired."

He nodded. "I would imagine so. If you'd told me you planned to visit I could have picked you up from the airport."

She waved a hand at him. "You know I despise being dependent on others to get me around. I wanted a rental anyway."

Shawn studied his mother. "True, but it's not like you to visit without warning. Not to mention Valentine's Day is well over two weeks away."

A sigh escaped his mother's lips. "The house is lonely without your father there. I couldn't stand it anymore. Grace is in Europe and Judy is so busy with the twins. Grant and his wife don't need me around adding more stress and Susie's still taking care of Darren after his surgery. I would only be in the way with any of the married children and Grace is too far away to visit," Miranda finished, tears glistening in her eyes. "I figured you wouldn't mind me coming. No need for both of us to be lonely."

Wrapping her in a comforting embrace, Shawn felt emotion clog his throat. It had only been two months since his father passed. While he called his mother often to check in on her, he hadn't considered how big and empty their house must feel to her. "It's okay, Mom. You're always welcome here." They ate their breakfast and discussed mundane little nothings to keep his mother's mind off her loneliness. "Are you sure you don't want me to stay?" Shawn asked as they cleared the table together. "I can reschedule my date. I'm sure Gladys would understand."

"Oh no, dear. You go on. It's about time you started dating someone and I really am quite exhausted after my journey."

"If you give me your keys, I'll just bring your bags in for you then."

Handing him a simple key ring, she said, "Don't open any of them. I have some surprises for you."

"And that's supposed to make me stay out of your bags?" Shawn teased.

Miranda smacked his arm. "Don't you spoil anything."

He laughed. "I won't, Mom. I'll be right back in." He walked out to see a blue sedan parked in his driveway. A chill breeze reminded him he'd neglected to put a coat on before going out. He quickly unlocked the car and gathered the two suitcases his mother had brought with her. Once inside again, he asked, "Shall I put these in the guest room for you?"

"That would be fine, dear."

Shawn set the suitcases down and then came back to the living room where his mother sat looking out the window. "Will you be okay while I'm gone?"

"Of course I will be. I can't get into too much trouble when I'm taking a nap," she added with a teasing grin.

He glanced at his watch. While there was still ample time before his date, his mother's impromptu visit put him in need of extra groceries. Grateful he'd put fresh linens on the guest bed only the week before, Shawn led his mother to her new room. "I'm going to go run some errands. Is there anything I can get for you while I'm out?"

"If it's not too much bother, some lemon tea would be much appreciated. I think I'm coming down with a cold."

He typed it into his phone. "Anything else?"

"I don't think so, dear. Just get whatever you would normally."

Chapter 8

Johnny wandered the aisles of the grocery store. His mother had sent him to run errands for her since she and the two little boys were down with some kind of respiratory infection. He didn't mind the excuse to get out of the house. The nervous energy building in him was fast reaching critical levels. Walking around the grocery store would help get his kind-of-sort-of-maybe-a-date out of his mind. Or at least, further back. He saw Coach Winston in the produce department. "Hi, Coach," he said.

Shawn glanced over. "Oh, hi, Johnny. Didn't expect you here."

"Mom's not feeling well, so I'm in charge of

stocking the pantry."

"I hope she gave you a list." Shawn winked. "Otherwise she might find her pantry full of soda and cheese balls."

"Coach, I'm hurt," Johnny replied, feigning offense. "You ought to know I'm the finest teen chef in Romance. I only allow quality ingredients in my pantry."

Shawn laughed as he eyed Johnny's cart of ramen, canned noodles, and soups. "Yes, I can see that. Hope your mom is better soon."

"Oh, she never stays down long. It's the little boys we're all worried about. They've got a real bad cold and Mom's worried it'll go to their lungs. How about you? What brings you to the store on this fine Saturday morning?"

"Not wanting my mother to think I'm too poor to keep my pantry stocked."

"Your mom is in town?" Johnny asked, surprised that Coach would plan a date while he had company.

Shawn nodded. "Showed up on my doorstep this morning."

"Wow, that's crazy. Hope it doesn't ruin your

plans." He also hoped he was being subtle enough that the coach would give away some details about this coming lunch date.

"Nah."

Johnny waited, but more information was not forthcoming. *Dang.* "Good to hear. Well, have a good weekend, Coach."

"You too, Johnny. Oh, get your mom and brothers some lemon tea. My mom swears by it. With enough honey added, the boys just might think they're getting a treat."

"Lemon tea," Johnny repeated, scrawling it on his list. "Thanks for the tip. See ya later." He moved away to finish his shopping. When a rock song sounded loudly from his pocket, he pulled out his phone before too many fellow shoppers could stare. The messaging icon blinked.

If my mother asks you, we're studying over lunch for our English test over Midsummer Night's Dream.

Johnny laughed to himself. "You could have used a lot less characters shortening that up, Rosenthal." *k*, he sent back.

Would it kill you to write out a full word? Just

one?

prbly

Imagining how irritated Stacie would be with him, he chuckled. What she didn't know was how cute she looked when flustered. Her cheeks flushed and her blue eyes blazed. Of course, she was beautiful when she wasn't mad at him too. But he couldn't help getting a rise out of her every now and again.

He finished gathering the items on his list, throwing a box of lemon tea in his cart at the last second, before heading to the check-out. He heard Coach Winston's voice a couple lanes over.

"I can't this afternoon. I have a lunch appointment and then I'll be spending the rest of the day with my mom."

"You're going to miss an afternoon with the guys to be with your mom? At your age?"

"Considering she just arrived, yes, that's exactly what I'm going to do." Johnny didn't miss the irritation in Coach's voice and wondered if he'd ever made his peers do push-ups when they frustrated him.

"Tough luck. Maybe next weekend, huh?"

"We'll see. Mom's going to be in town for a

while. I don't think I'll be getting out much until she heads back home."

Interesting, Johnny thought before turning his attention to the cashier as he put items on the conveyor belt. A display of simple flower arrangements caught his eye. *Just a study session, Rosenthal? I'll show you.* "Just a second. Can I grab one of those bouquets real quick?"

The older gentleman smiled. "Sure, son."

Johnny picked the least wilted of the bunch and finished his purchase. Once at the car, he prayed none of his younger brothers would destroy the flowers before he left for his date. If the weather was a little nicer he might leave them in the car, but he didn't think that was a good option either. He drove home and was greeted by unusual quiet. He saw his mom sitting in the living room, holding a finger to her mouth.

"I just got the boys to sleep," she whispered. Her green eyes fell on the bouquet of flowers in Johnny's hand. "Something for your date?"

"Yeah. Think she'll like them?"

Chuckling, his mother said, "I'm sure she'll think they're lovely."

Johnny looked around. The two youngest boys were asleep on the couch, but none of his other brothers were in sight. "Where's everyone else?"

"Your dad came home early and took the healthy kids to the roller skate rink. He thought that might give the little ones and me a chance to rest." She coughed and then looked at Johnny. "You look worried. Is everything okay?"

"Yeah." When she raised an eyebrow at him, he sighed. "Do you think it's weird that she's telling her mom this is just a study session?"

His mom was quiet a moment. "Johnny, not all teens are close to their parents. She might not be comfortable telling her mom she's going on a date with anyone. With her mom being recently divorced, it might feel like a betrayal of some kind."

"But it's not her fault her dad was a jerk."

"No, but our feelings aren't always dictated by logic." She smiled. "Especially when we're teenagers. I don't think she's trying to keep you in the 'just friends' category, if that's what you're worried about. And even if she is, you are just in high school. No need to plan out your future together just yet."

"Mom," Johnny groaned.

She laughed and then coughed sharply. "Anyway, you should probably get ready for your date and I need to get some rest while they're sleeping," she said, nodding at the two toddlers.

"I'll finish bringing in the groceries. I saw Coach Winston at the store. He suggested lemon tea for you and the boys. I went ahead and got a box. Would you like me to make you some before I go?"

"If I'm still awake," his mother answered with a smile. "Thanks for all your help. I got pretty lucky when God sent you to me."

"I'm the lucky one," Johnny said, kissing her cheek. "How many other moms do you think practice football with their sons?"

"More than you might think."

Johnny laughed and went back out to his car to bring in the groceries. Once he'd finished putting everything away, he checked on his mom. She was sleeping soundly on the sofa. He put the change, and an extra twenty for the additional things he'd gotten, on the table with the box of lemon tea before going to his room to change. The first piece of dating advice his father had ever given him was to always dress to impress. The second was to treat your date better than you would treat a princess. "You can't go wrong if you're showing respect and genuine admiration."

"Sure hope you're right, Dad," Johnny said. Convinced he was as ready as he could be, he glanced at his watch. Eleven thirty-five. The drive to Stacie's would only take five minutes, but his mother insisted being early was infinitely better than being late. Inclined to agree with her, he left a short note for his mom before walking out the door.

Chapter 9

Stacie went through her closet three times before finally deciding upon a periwinkle sweater dress and her favorite wool tights. Accessories took even longer to choose, though she immediately grabbed her white belt to give the dress a little more shape. When she finally put on the sparkling snowflake earrings and pendant, she knew Johnny would be arriving soon. Grabbing her large white shoulder bag, she looked in the mirror. "This isn't a date," she told her reflection. "It's a reconnaissance mission. Yeah." She took a deep breath and turned to the door.

A voice in her head laughed as she stepped out of her room just as the doorbell rang. She heard

Johnny's deep voice. "Is Stacie here?"

"I'm sure she'll be down soon. Flowers for a study session?"

Flowers? Stacie thought, warmth flooding her at the sweet gesture.

"Um, yeah, we're doing a…poetry unit. So they seemed fitting."

"Uh-huh." Stacie could tell by her mother's tone she didn't believe him. Her heart sank as Gladys continued, "Stacie's a very bright girl."

"Yes, ma'am. Like her mother, I'm sure."

"That's kind of you to say. She's worked hard to be the best in her classes. She's got a bright future."

Mom, what are you doing?

"I'm sure a football player like yourself understands the need for discipline and determination. Stacie can go anywhere. Do anything she wants, if she keeps her focus where it should be."

Stacie wanted to scream. What was her mother thinking? She imagined the nosedive her social life was about to take when Johnny let the other guys at Romance Valley High know Stacie had bigger, better things than dating on her mind. Then she heard Johnny clear his throat.

"Mrs. Rosenthal, I don't intend to become a distraction to your daughter, and frankly, I don't think I could if I tried. I've never met a more diligent student or determined person. It's why I admire her so much."

Color rushed into Stacie's face and she decided she'd eavesdropped long enough. She walked loudly down the stairs. "Hi, Johnny," she said, hoping her walk had given her cheeks time to cool.

"Hi. I brought some flowers for our study session," he said, winking at her.

"How thoughtful!" Why was it suddenly so warm? She knew why. Johnny's grin was turning her insides to jelly. He might think he couldn't distract her, but that was far from the truth. "Mom, would you be willing to put these on my desk for me?"

Gladys glanced from Stacie to Johnny again. She sighed. "Sure. Make sure you're home before suppertime."

"Don't worry, Mrs. Rosenthal. I'll have her home on time." He led Stacie out to his car and opened her door. "Your carriage, milady."

"Poetry unit? Really?" She smirked as she got in the car.

"Hey, I was on the spot," Johnny replied. He closed her door and walked around to the driver's side.

"Didn't you get my text?"

"Oh, I got it. But would it be so terrible for me to take you on a date?" he asked.

Stacie didn't answer right away while Johnny started driving around the block. Her mother's words echoed in her ears. "About my mom…"

Johnny shook his head and gave a dismissive wave of his hand. "Don't worry about it, Rosenthal."

"No, you need to understand. Dad was a football player. She…"

"She's trying to protect you," Johnny interrupted with a kind smile. "I get it. She's got good reason to worry. I am pretty distracting," he said with a wink.

You have no idea, Stacie thought, though she simply laughed. "So what's the plan, Master Distracter?"

He gave her a heart-melting grin. "I like that. I think I'll make it my new gaming persona."

Stacie laughed again. "Really, though, what's the plan?"

"We wait for your mom to leave the house and

then follow at a safe distance wherever she goes. I happened to bump into Coach at the grocery store. He mentioned that his mother is in town."

"That's crazy. Do you think it will mess with our plans?"

"Potentially," Johnny admitted, watching Stacie's mother pull out of their driveway. "But I'd say finding out how today goes will give us a pretty good indication." They were quiet for a moment and Johnny looked her over. "You look nice, especially for a study session," he added with a wink.

A pleased blush crept up her neck. "I guess perhaps I did overdress for the occasion, didn't I?"

"I don't mind. You look beautiful."

Stacie turned her attention to the window. "How is it that Coach is still single? The man practically oozes confidence on the field."

Johnny chuckled. "We all do. We have to. If you don't look and act confident, the other team will smell your fear."

"Isn't that a little primitive?"

He shrugged. "Maybe, but it's true. Football players, especially the good ones, learn to put on that persona so we don't get eaten alive. I would guess

Coach has always been the shy, quiet type and just kept it hidden when he was playing. Just like he keeps it hidden during practice or when we're at a game. But you have him in class. Have you ever heard him raise his voice?"

"Only when Millie Barnes nearly caught her bangs on fire," Stacie admitted, giggling at the memory. "That was probably the best chemistry lesson ever."

Johnny laughed. "I'll bet." He watched Gladys pull into the parking lot of Della's Diner. "Well, this will complicate things somewhat. How are we supposed to keep an eye on them without being conspicuous?"

"Easy." Stacie pulled her English book out of her bag. "I came prepared. All we have to do is pick a table somewhat nearby and then start reading whatever stuff we're doing in class right now. It is lunchtime, after all, and Della's is the best place for lunch."

"Certainly better than the cafeteria," Johnny agreed. "That was a good idea, bringing your English book."

Stacie's blue eyes sparkled as she grinned. "If

you're going to run a fake, you have to make it convincing, Belcarro."

He laughed. "Got me there." He drove them around the parking lot and picked a spot away from Gladys' car.

They waited a couple minutes before Stacie said, "Shall we go in?"

She started to open her door and Johnny put a hand on her arm. "Please let me get the door. If my dad finds out I had a girl on a date, even a study session, and she opened her own door, he'd have me running laps all night!"

Surprised, Stacie raised an eyebrow. "Really?"

"Probably not, but better safe than sorry. If you can wait ten seconds, I'll get your door for you."

Stacie waited, impressed that Johnny's father had taught him to be a gentleman. Her dad never bothered to teach her anything about dating or guys in general, leaving that to her mom. The divorce left Gladys so distracted and hurt she hadn't taken time to tell Stacie much either. Other than the occasional, "Boys are trouble, stay away from them."

Johnny offered her his hand. "Coming, Rosenthal?"

"That took you twelve seconds, Johnny," she teased, though she accepted his hand. The warmth spread from her fingers to her heart. "You might have to run laps after all for keeping a lady waiting."

"I won't tell if you won't."

She laughed. They walked into the diner and she spotted a booth that would be close enough to eavesdrop but hopefully prevent them from being noticed. Tipping her head in that direction, Johnny nodded and led the way to the booth. Stacie surveyed the table her mom was sitting at with Coach Winston. A lovely bouquet of flowers set to the side made her smile. At least Coach had come with his A game. She slid into the booth and Johnny slid in next to her. She pulled out her English book, just in case.

A waitress came over. "Welcome to Della's Diner. What can I get for you to drink?"

Stacie looked up. "Oh, just water, please."

Johnny raised an eyebrow at her. "No one comes to Della's for 'just water.' How about two raspberry lemonades?"

"That okay with you, hon?" the waitress directed to Stacie.

"Yes, that's fine." When the waitress walked

away, she rolled her eyes at Johnny. "Seriously? I like drinking water. It's good for you."

"Live a little. One raspberry lemonade won't kill you."

Stacie gave an irritated sigh before turning her attention to the menu. She'd almost made her choice when a loud voice said, "Hey, Belcarro! Fancy seeing you here."

She looked up in panic as Marco punched Johnny's arm. Johnny was smooth as ever as he said, "Hey, Marco, so good of you to finally join us."

"Huh?"

"The study session, remember?"

After Johnny gave a significant nod to Coach Winston's table, Marco smiled. "Oh yeah, I almost forgot. Hope you haven't started without me."

"We were just about to order lunch," Stacie said, forcing herself not to look at the table her mother was sitting at. Any hope of their presence going unnoticed was gone. But, if she didn't look at their table, her mom might think it was merely a coincidence. *Yeah, right.*

"Good thing, I'm starved," Marco said, sitting down at the table with them. He lowered his voice,

"They're not looking anymore. What's going on?"

"Well, we were trying to keep an eye on how their first date goes. You kind of spoiled everything," Johnny retorted.

"No, I haven't. You've got an English book there. We study, spy on Coach, and get to eat the best burgers in town. Triple win there."

"Except you're not in our class, Marco," Stacie pointed out.

"So? All the English teachers teach the same stuff anyway."

Stacie glanced at Johnny, who simply shrugged. She sighed. "Well, let's start with Shakespeare's sonnets."

Chapter 10

Shawn looked up from his menu as Gladys scowled at the table of teenagers. "Is something wrong?" he asked.

"Isn't it obvious?" she hissed.

He blinked. "I guess not."

"They're spying on us," she replied, her voice low enough the other table wouldn't hear. "Study session my foot. Why, when I get home that girl…"

"Gladys, you don't know that they're spying on us," Shawn interrupted. "Della's is one of the most popular diners in town. And it's a great atmosphere for studying." He heard Stacie's voice reading a poem of some kind. "It certainly sounds like they're studying."

She narrowed her eyes. "I suppose so."

"Relax, Gladys, and pretend they're not here."

"Easy for you to say."

He shrugged. "No, not really. I've got a group of jokers right now and Marco's the worst of them. I guarantee you I'll hear about this on Monday. They'll want to know who the charming woman at my table was." Shawn smiled as Gladys relaxed. "Don't worry about them. Let them study whatever it is Stacie is reading."

"That would be Shakespeare."

"Yeah, well, English was never my strong suit," Shawn replied with a grin. "I did much better in the sciences."

"How did you end up playing football? It seems that brains and brawn don't usually mix."

Shawn laughed. "My mother would tell you they don't mix at all. Dad was a football player and so I played football too. It was something he wanted and I enjoyed it too. Coaching seemed like the best way to keep a foot in both worlds. I can teach science and be as brainy as I want while still enjoying a good football game now and again. Plus it gives me the chance to interact with young people, which I wouldn't have had going into research or the NFL."

"Could you have gone professional?" Gladys asked, her eyes wide.

"Not as a starting player, no. And probably not even as a bench warmer," he added. "As fascinating as research is, I didn't want to spend my whole life in a laboratory. So I decided I would teach. Probably the best decision I ever made."

She smiled. "I thought about teaching. But then I had Stacie and I wanted to stay home with her. She needed so much care."

"Really?"

Gladys nodded. "For as independent and headstrong as she is now, she didn't start out that way. She was seven weeks early. Spent the first three weeks of her life in the NICU trying to figure out what it meant to breathe and eat. The next two months she needed pretty much constant care at home. I had absolutely no time to myself because Jesse needed to be able to focus on his classwork. I got so behind in my own classes that I failed every single one of them."

"Shouldn't your professors have given you some

leeway?" Shawn asked, angry that she'd been put at such a disadvantage. "You'd just had a baby, and a preemie at that."

"Perhaps they should have," she said with a shrug. "But they didn't and I didn't fight for any. I knew Stacie needed me and that was enough for me. The first few years of her life we spent in and out of the hospital, mostly with problems developed from being so early. I was so busy with Stacie that I never took the time to go back to school. By the time she was well enough, I just didn't want to. Since Jesse left, I sometimes wish I'd finished my degree. It would have given me better footing."

"Not necessarily, Gladys," he replied. "A lot has changed in the last sixteen years. Not that you should let that deter you," he said quickly when she frowned at him. "There's nothing to say you can't finish that degree now and learn all the new information and such."

"Oh, but my budget does," she admitted. "That's part of why I'm tutoring. That reminds me. During our last conversation you mentioned business cards." She pulled a baggie from her purse. "I just picked these up from the print shop yesterday. Do you think they'll work?"

He looked over the card she handed him. It was a little too feminine for his taste with the pink floral background. But her name was prominently displayed along with a phone number and email address. She'd even listed the subjects she tutored on the back of the card. "They look great. I'm sure this will be very helpful for students looking for some extra help."

"You don't think they're too girly, do you?"

Shawn laughed nervously. "Gladys, I don't think there's a good answer for that. Pink is definitely not my color, but that really doesn't matter. They look professional and they reflect your personality. That makes them perfect."

She blushed and smiled. "You think so?"

"I think so." Their food arrived and he smiled. "Dig in."

The meal continued with much laughter and soon he'd forgotten all about the teenagers sitting in the table catty-corner to his. Gladys agreed to split dessert with him, which was good because the ice cream-topped-brownie was far too much for him to eat by himself. "It's a good thing I don't eat here more often," he said as they finished. "I'd have to get a new belt if I did."

Gladys laughed. "Are you saying you've got a sweet tooth?"

"Guilty as charged." He looked at Gladys and half-wished his mother hadn't come to visit. He couldn't justify spending every evening with Gladys when his mother needed him too. "Thank you for coming to have lunch with me."

"I have to admit, I've never been asked on a date via flower delivery before," Gladys replied with a teasing grin. "I almost decided not to come."

"What convinced you to change your mind?"

"The flowers were too beautiful to resist."

Shawn chuckled. "I'll have to add that to my list of acceptable dating practices." He covered Gladys' hand with his own. "I had a great time this afternoon," he said, nerves building up inside him like frenzied butterflies.

"I did too," she said, her smile dazzling him and chasing away any logical thoughts he might have had.

"Um, I." He swallowed down his nerves. "I'd like to have dinner with you sometime, if you're up for it."

A tiny frown creased her brow. "Well..."

"I make pretty good steaks. Maybe you could come to my place for dinner, say Tuesday?"

"Stacie volunteers at the animal shelter on Tuesdays and we always get tacos at El Torero."

"Would Thursday be better for you?"

She hesitated and Shawn braced himself for disappointment. "I don't know. I'll have to check my schedule. Stacie sometimes has things going on that I forget about. Especially now that she's helping Dr. Foster nurse a family of Great Pyrenees dogs back to health."

"Sure, I understand." The waitress came back with his card. After getting it back into his wallet, he said, "I'll walk you out to your car." Shawn helped Gladys into her coat before walking with her to the door. He stole a glance at the table of teenagers. The sight of Stacie being dwarfed by Johnny and Marco brought a smile to his face. Marco caught his eye and gave a roguish wink. Returning it with his best glare, Shawn continued outside with Gladys. The wind had picked up, biting through his thick coat.

When he and Gladys arrived at her car, she

placed the flowers on the passenger's seat and then turned back to him. "I really did have a nice time with you. If Thursday doesn't work out, you've got my number."

"Do I?" Shawn asked.

She handed him a stack of business cards. "You do now. Don't give all of those to your students." Gladys got in the car. "Goodbye, Shawn."

"Goodbye." He watched her drive away before getting in his vehicle to drive home. She hadn't said no to a second date, but she hadn't said yes either. It might be a very long few weeks with his mom if he couldn't convince the PTO mom to go out with him again.

~*~

"Argh," Stacie growled once her mom was out of the diner. "Now what?"

"Well, she didn't say no," Johnny pointed out.

"Yeah, but she didn't say yes either," she fumed. "I usually try to keep Thursdays open so I can spend extra time on homework, and Mom knows that."

Marco scratched the stubbly growth on his chin. "Then it's time for Coach to get a little sneaky."

"How?" Johnny asked.

"Tuesday is taco night at El Torero, yeah?" he asked Stacie.

"Yeah, we've been doing it for years. It used to be on Fridays, but after…" she let her voice trail off. "Well, we just do it on Tuesdays now."

"What time are you normally there?"

"I get done volunteering at five thirty. So it's normally about five forty-five when we get there."

"Perfect, we get Coach to go at five thirty and wait for you guys to arrive. He just happens to be there and he can just happen to invite you guys to sit with him."

"No good," Johnny said.

"Why not?" Stacie asked.

"Because of you."

"I beg your pardon?"

"You're his student. He can't be seen to show any kind of favoritism because kids talk and teenagers are jerks. Maybe that's part of why your mom is being hesitant. I mean, there aren't rules or anything about dating your student's parent, I don't think, but think how that might look if your grades improved."

Stacie rolled her eyes. "I've already got an A in

his class and have since day one. No one would think anything and anyone who did could take a look at my grade reports. Besides, your logic would make more sense if he was the one hesitating."

"You don't hesitate when you're in it to win it," Marco said. "It was nice to see him show a little confidence off-field."

"But that near rejection might ruin it." Johnny thought for a minute. "I think you're right, Marco. We've got to convince Coach to be waiting at El Torero for Stacie's mom. And if Stacie doesn't mind, maybe I can just happen to be there for another study session."

"I think that would be suspicious, not that another study session wouldn't be welcomed," she added. "My friend Marisol works there. If she's got a shift that night, maybe I can convince her to take her dinner break while I'm there and then Mom and Coach could have dinner without me and no one will have any reason to suspect he's showing favorites."

Johnny frowned. "Just one problem. How do we convince him to do it?"

"You leave that to me," Marco said, a broad grin spreading over his face.

Chapter 11

The delicious aroma of fresh-baked cookies filled Shawn's nose as he walked into his house. He went to the kitchen, where his mother pulled a batch of cookies out of the oven. "I see you're up from your nap."

"And you're back from your date just in time for milk and cookies," Miranda replied with a smile. "How did it go?"

"Great. We had a great time," he said, trying not to think about how it ended.

"But?"

"But what?" he asked.

"You look unhappy, so something must have

happened." She set down the kitchen gloves before piercing him with an intense stare.

"I'm not unhappy, Mom." Shawn took a moment to gather his thoughts. "Dating her is going to be even harder than I imagined."

"What makes you think so?"

"Well, for one thing she didn't say yes to a second date."

"One rejection doesn't mean you should give up," Miranda said.

"She didn't say no."

A puzzled look crossed her face. "I'm confused. If she didn't say no and she didn't say yes, what did she say?"

"Essentially, 'We'll see.' That's like the dating kiss of death," Shawn replied.

Miranda laughed. "Not hardly. If she'd said, 'Oh, you're a great friend,' that would be the dating kiss of death. Really, you need to get out more."

"I'm trying to."

She hugged him and tapped his nose as she'd done since he was a boy. "I know, Shawn. Just keep trying. Tell me about the good parts of the date."

Shawn spent the next several minutes discussing

his afternoon with Gladys. "I don't know, Mom. It's as if she's interested in dating but not interested at the same time," he said after telling her about the business card. "I just don't get it."

"Women are confusing creatures, I'm afraid. Especially women who've been hurt. Poor Gladys has had many challenges, from what you've said. And it sounds like she had to deal with most of them alone. The fact that she gave you her card and told you to call her if things didn't work out for the day you wanted tells me she's interested in dating you. You just might have to change your gameplay a little."

He sighed. "I was afraid of that."

~*~

Monday afternoon, Shawn wasn't at all surprised during winter weights when Marco asked loudly, "So, Coach, who were you having lunch with Saturday?"

"Ooh, Coach had a date?"

"Was she pretty?"

"What's her name?"

"Details, Coach!"

"All right," Shawn said, holding his hands up,

"all right. If you want information, you better work on your weight training. I want one rep from each of you before I say anything." He watched the athletes train, ensuring that they kept their good form. When the last finished, he said, "I had lunch with Mrs. Rosenthal on Saturday. It was merely a casual lunch, nothing for you to get excited about."

"You sure about that, Coach?" Marco asked with his characteristic grin.

"Another rep."

"Aw, man."

Shawn wasn't sure he wanted to deal with advice concerning his love life from teenagers. It was bad enough Valentine's Day was approaching and the city was going crazy with the decorations. Even though he was used to the sudden infestation of pink and red hearts, this year seemed worse than before. Maybe that was because this year he actually had someone he wanted to celebrate the holiday with. Someone who might not be interested in him.

"Okay, we're done. So, are you sure?" Marco repeated. "I don't normally take flowers to a casual lunch."

Resisting the urge to toss a weight at the boy's

head, Shawn said, "Whether or not I am really isn't any of your business."

"Aw, come on, Coach," Garrett said. "You've never kept secrets from us before."

"Yeah, we're all guys here," Brady added.

"Hey!" Misty snapped. "Not all of us."

"Sorry," Brady called. "Most of us. You could get lots of good advice."

"That's what I'm afraid of. Next rep." While the students lifted weights, Shawn said, "In the interest of keeping a good rapport with you, yes, I'd like to have a closer relationship with Mrs. Rosenthal. However, that doesn't mean I need a bunch of hormonally charged, inexperienced, half-grown teens giving me advice."

"Pretty sure that was an insult, Coach," one of the boys wheezed.

"Ease off the weight, Sanders," Shawn replied. "You shouldn't be breathing that hard."

"This cold has my asthma flaring up."

"Exactly. Reduce your weight. Your dad would skin me alive if I worked you into an asthma attack."

"We could help you," one of the three girls participating said.

"How would your advice be any better than ours?" Brady demanded.

"Easy, we're actually girls," another retorted.

"It's a generous offer, Jazzlyn" Shawn said, heading off an argument, "but hormonally charged girls aren't any better than hormonally charged boys. Simple biology there."

They rolled their eyes. "Whatever."

The girls began chatting with each other as Marco said, "I understand Mrs. Rosenthal and her daughter have dinner at El Torero on Tuesdays."

Blast it all, they were spying! Shawn narrowed his eyes. "How would you know that?"

"We've seen them there before," Johnny replied. Shawn saw through the attempted cover easily but decided not to pursue it.

"If it were me, Coach," Marco said, "I'd be waiting there for her. Girls like surprises, right, Misty?"

"What kind of surprises?" she asked. "I wasn't listening."

"Dinner."

She breathed out as she lowered a weight. "As long as I don't have to cook it, yeah, dinner is a great surprise. Is that an offer?" She lifted it once again.

Marco shrugged. "Sure. You and me on Friday?"

"Sounds good. But chocolate is an even better surprise."

"And both would be the best surprise of all if you're trying to get a girl to like you," Jazzlyn added.

Marco grinned. "So there you have it. Dinner and chocolate. Unless you'd rather spend yet another Valentine's Day in Romance by yourself."

Shawn scowled. "Focus on your weights, Polo."

The boys laughed but continued their weight training. As much as he tried not to, Shawn couldn't help feeling the sting of Marco's challenge. Truth be told, he didn't want to spend Valentine's Day with only his mother for company. But that too presented a challenge. He couldn't leave her alone in her grief, and most women didn't really want their date's mother along for the ride. But the idea of surprising Gladys at El Torero did have a certain appeal. It would show Gladys that he was paying attention to her and was genuinely interested. Or it would look like stalking. Maybe not if he added a box of chocolates from Cicely's Caramel and Chocolate Company.

An inner debate started in his head while Marco said, "Five thirty would probably be the best time to go."

"More lifting, less talking," Shawn barked. He moved around the room, helping various students with their technique. He stopped for a while by Marco and Johnny, who were using equipment next to each other. While Johnny appeared to be working hard, Marco lifted his weights with ease. "I think you could add a little more weight to that, Polo. You don't seem too challenged by what you have."

"Maybe next time, Coach. I'm taking an easy day."

"Just remember, you only get one per week."

"Right."

As he moved on, Shawn heard Marco say, "Told you it would work." *What are those boys up to now?*

Chapter 12

Gladys was surprised to find Stacie outside waiting for her when she arrived at Finding Forever. "Is everything okay?" she asked as her daughter got in the car.

"Yeah. Cha-Cha and the puppies are getting along great. You should have seen them, so cute and snuggly!" An excited squeal escaped her. "Frenchy's fur is starting to come back in, so she doesn't look so scrawny and her mama's milk is making her a fat, happy pup."

"So no more bottle feeds, huh?" Gladys waited until Stacie's seatbelt was on before pulling out of the parking lot.

"Well, because they are so malnourished, Dr. Foster wants them supplemented with the bottles until they're looking healthier. Zuko is not a fan though. He kept trying to wriggle away from me."

"Will that be a problem?"

"Of all the pups, he is the healthiest, surprisingly enough, so probably not. Anyway, I was outside because they were all asleep when I finished walking the other dogs and I didn't want to disturb them with extra cuddles." Stacie smiled as they reached El Torero, a little family-owned Mexican restaurant on Douglass Street.

They walked inside and were greeted by Stacie's friend, Marisol Alvarez. "Buenas tardes."

"Buenas tardes," Stacie replied, once again grateful she'd chosen to take Spanish classes at school. "¿Cómo estas?"

"Muy bien, gracias. Señor Winston te espera." Marisol motioned for them to follow her.

"What?" Gladys asked.

Stacie's eyes twinkled mischievously as she said, "Sorry, I didn't catch it."

Marisol snorted, confirming that Stacie absolutely did catch it. Gladys frowned.

"Anastasia..."

"Good evening, Gladys."

Her breath hitched. Shawn looked incredible wearing a dress shirt nearly the same cerulean shade as his eyes and a smile that made her knees wobble. A small bouquet of flowers rested on the table next to a box from Cicely's. When this man decided to impress someone, he went all the way. "Hello, Shawn."

"Marisol, I hate to intrude on their date. Have you had your dinner break yet?" Stacie asked, winking.

"No, I haven't. Why don't you come sit with me towards the back and then your mom can enjoy her evening?"

"See ya, Mom."

Gladys watched Stacie and Marisol giggle their way to the back of the restaurant. "I don't know how she did it, but I swear I'm going to ground that girl for a month," she said, accepting the seat Shawn offered her.

Shawn chuckled. "I don't think she's entirely to blame. I've got a pair of football players backing her up." He gave her another dazzling smile. "I'm glad they did, though. I hope you don't mind me being here."

"You didn't think it might look creepy?" Gladys asked, trying not to forgive him for encouraging the teens.

"I figured since you told me where you'd be, it was a subtle invitation," he said with a nervous smile. "And chocolate makes everything better, right?"

Unable to keep the frustrated charade going, Gladys laughed. "Well, yes, chocolate is rather magical that way. And more flowers? I could almost open my own floral shop."

"Nah, I haven't gotten you that many. You do like them, though, right?"

"Yes, I'm teasing you," she said, noting the worry in his eyes. "Flowers, chocolate, surprise dates. How are you still single?"

"Well, my mother could give you a whole slew of answers to that question. But I'll settle for I hadn't met the right person yet."

Gladys blushed. "I see."

After the waitress took their orders, Shawn reached over to take Gladys' hand. "Look, I know you're trying to take things slow. You've been hurt and I imagine you're not eager for a repeat experience. But please believe me when I say I would never intentionally hurt you. We can take this as slow as you want. Just give me the chance to show you that my intentions are genuine."

"And just what are your intentions?" she asked, almost afraid to hear the answer.

"For now? To enjoy an evening with the most beautiful woman in Romance, enjoying the best tacos in town."

The sincerity in his tone warmed her heart. His thumb made lazy circles on the back of her hand, sending tingling currents through her arm. She hadn't been so pampered in a long time. Realizing he was still waiting for an answer, she smiled. "All right, Shawn. We'll see where this goes."

"Good. Then you and Stacie can come to my house for dinner Thursday."

"Aren't you worried about what that might do to Stacie?"

Shawn shook his head. "If you're worried about people thinking it's favoritism, I've thought of that. But she's had near perfect grades since the beginning of the year. And I do enough with my football players, most of whom can't boast Stacie's average score, that I can't really see people making the complaint. But, I'm willing to maintain a more casual relationship through the end of the school year, if that would make you more comfortable."

Gladys smiled. "I think dinner Thursday sounds wonderful, though Stacie is sixteen and can fend for herself when needed."

"I figured she could, but to be completely honest with you, my mother is visiting me right now and I think she and Stacie would get along really well. I know Mom could use the company."

"Oh, I'm so sorry to take you away from family."

Shawn waved her worries away. "She insisted I come on my own tonight. You see, I didn't realize she was coming until she arrived on my doorstep Saturday morning. My father passed away last fall."

"Yes, I remember the email from the principal. I am sorry about that."

Nodding, Shawn continued, "Mom felt too lonely at the house, especially with Valentine's Day approaching. Since I'm the only single child in visiting distance, she booked herself a flight, rented a car, and invited herself over."

Gladys laughed. "She sounds like quite a character."

"Oh, she is. But I know she would be thrilled to meet you and Stacie. Tonight she wanted to give us a chance to have a talk without interference."

"If you told her about Stacie, wouldn't she have realized I wasn't coming alone anyway?"

Shawn chuckled. "I told her and she said, 'A bright girl like that probably already has a plan in place, just in case.' I'm not going to argue with Mom, especially not when she's right."

"Stacie is a special girl," Gladys said, pride filling her. "And far too bright for her own good."

"We need more like her."

~*~

Stacie watched the couple. "Thanks for doing this, Marisol. I definitely owe you one."

"No, you don't," she replied. "Having company other than my brother during my dinner break is definitely payment enough."

Laughing, Stacie said, "Well, everything looks to be going well. I'd say at this point it's just a matter of time."

"Hopefully it will be longer rather than shorter."

Stacie frowned. "Why would you want that?"

"Because I can't wait to get my hands on Brady Sanders," she said, rubbing her hands together. "He's been teasing me since we were kids and this would be the ultimate revenge. Putting make up and sparkles all over him for the whole school to see? Perfection!"

Stacie giggled. "True. But I suppose that means I give up prom with Johnny."

Marisol snorted. "I don't think he's going to let you get away from him that easily."

Heat rushed into Stacie's face. "What do you mean?"

"Come on, Stacie, you're not that blind," Marisol retorted. "Johnny's been trying to get the courage to ask you out since we were freshmen. Now that he's managed one date, he's not going to give up without a fight."

"Have you heard from Annie recently?" Stacie asked, turning the conversation away from herself. She half-listened as Marisol described how their fellow cheerleader was healing after a car accident that left her with two broken legs and a fractured collarbone. From her vantage point, Gladys looked relaxed and happy. Happier than she'd been in a long time. Stacie was glad. If anyone in the world deserved to be happy, it was her mom. Her phone buzzing drew her attention.

Stacie, your mom isn't answering her phone. Are you two okay?

A wicked grin spread over her face. "You want to talk about perfect revenge? Guess who just texted me?"

"Johnny?"

"No. My dad. Mom isn't answering her phone and he wants to know if we're okay."

Marisol squealed and moved closer to Stacie. "Ooooh, I want to see this exchange."

We're fine, Stacie typed. *Mom's on a date, and I'm with a friend. Sorry you missed us.*

"Sorry, not sorry," Marisol giggled.

The phone buzzed just seconds after she hit send. *What do you mean she's on a date?*

You didn't really think you were the only one allowed to move on, did you? She's on a date. Get over it. Anger burned in Stacie's chest and filled her mouth with a metallic taste. Tears pricked her eyes, but she ignored them.

Marisol put her arms around Stacie's shoulders and squeezed gently. "At least Coach isn't going to break her heart."

"I sure hope not. I don't think Mom could take it."

"Don't worry, amiga. Coach Winston has got to be the world's biggest teddy bear trapped in a football player's body."

Chapter 13

Despite her insistence that she'd rather stay at home, Stacie dressed nicely for dinner with Coach Winston and her mom. "His mother is in town and could use some company," Gladys told her. "Her husband passed away recently and I'm sure you'd be able to lift her spirits so much with your enthusiasm and zest for life."

"But isn't this supposed to be a date?"

"Family dates are a thing too, you know. We used to have a lot of them when you were younger," Gladys replied.

Stacie sat in the car and tried not to pout. At least she had her cell phone with her. She wouldn't be able to completely die of boredom. Maybe Johnny would text her.

"What's got you looking so grumpy?" Gladys asked. "It's not like you to be slouchy."

She sat up straighter. "Johnny asked me out."

"Why does that upset you? I thought you liked Johnny."

"Because he asked me to go out with him on Saturday, and I'll be at Dad's house. Couldn't I skip? Just this weekend? He's going to be mad at me anyway after Tuesday's fiasco." Stacie's last text sparked several ignored phone calls until they got home and Gladys answered her phone. Stacie couldn't remember the last time she'd heard her parents argue like that. Though she appreciated her mom taking her side, it hadn't saved her from a lecture on being respectful, and she just knew she would hear about it again during her weekend visit.

Gladys sighed. "I'm sorry, hon. I know the custody arrangement isn't ideal, but once you're eighteen it's up to you who you visit and how often and when."

"That birthday can't come fast enough," Stacie grumbled.

With a tight laugh Gladys replied, "It'll come faster than I'm ready for."

"I'll always visit you, Mom."

Gladys smiled, though it faded as she said, "Stacie, I know you're angry at your father and you have every right to be. I'm angry too. But, I hope you'll be able to forgive him enough to stay in touch with him as well. For all his flaws, he is still your father and he does love you."

Stacie snorted. "Whatever, Mom."

"I'm serious, Stacie. Don't alienate him, no matter how you might feel about him right now. If you do, I promise someday you'll regret it."

Stacie turned back toward the window, choosing not to respond. The silence in the car was broken only by the music playing on the local radio station.

"Did you hear the *Romance Is Dead* segment this morning?" Gladys asked. "Sounds like our poor DJ had quite the breakup."

"Yeah, Coach Winston always has the radio on for the start of class."

Gladys turned to Stacie as they pulled into the driveway of Shawn's house. "Listen, Stacie, I know you and your friends have been trying to set us up, and don't even try that innocent look with me. But if you don't really want me to pursue a relationship with him, just say the word."

Stacie laughed. "Mom, I wouldn't try to set you up with anyone I didn't think was a good fit for you and our family. You deserve some happiness. So quit worrying about what I think and just see where this goes. It's wonderful to see you smiling again." She watched her mom glance in the rearview mirror and fluff her hair. "You look great, Mom. Come on, let's go find out just how good Coach Winston's steaks really are." She got out of the car and walked with her mom up the little path to the front door. Stacie looked around. The yard looked well cared for and the house clean, though much smaller than she would have expected. She knocked on the door.

A smiling woman opened it. "Oh, you must be Stacie and you," she turned, "are Gladys, right?"

"Yes, it's a pleasure to meet you," Gladys replied.

"I'm Miranda. Shawn is out in the backyard finishing the steaks. Why don't you girls come with me and we'll have some cocoa while we're waiting? No sense in all of us freezing outside." They followed her into the house while she said, "Do you like cinnamon?"

"Oh, yes!" Stacie replied eagerly, the scent wafting through the air.

"Good. This is my favorite type of cocoa." Miranda ladled some into a mug from a small slow cooker. She placed a cinnamon stick in the mug and handed it to Stacie. "Use that to stir." She got a mug prepared for Gladys and for herself before showing them to a tiny table. "Hopefully we won't feel too crowded. I've been trying to convince Shawn he needs a bigger table, but he won't listen to me." She shook her head with a sigh. "Children can be so stubborn."

Gladys laughed. "I can certainly relate."

Stacie scowled until she took a sip of the cocoa. Rich, warm, and spiced with cinnamon, she was certain she'd never had cocoa quite so decadent before. "This is amazing!"

"Much better than packets, eh?" Miranda said with a wink.

"Infinitely better," Stacie replied. "How do you make it?"

"Oh, it's a simple matter of milk, chocolate, and

cinnamon sticks. I'll give the recipe to your mom before you ladies leave. Then you can enjoy it anytime you want. Unless, of course, you'd rather I keep the recipe for you and then you'd have an excuse to come visit me."

Coach Winston walked in with a steaming plate of steaks. "Don't let her convince you she's lonely here," he said with a teasing grin. "Otherwise you'll never have another moment of peace for as long as she's here."

They laughed and talked as the meal progressed. Stacie watched her mom interact with Coach Winston. They looked perfect together. She caught Miranda's eye and was surprised when the woman winked at her. "Stacie, dear, would you like to come help me bring something from my room?"

Pleased to have a fellow conspirator, Stacie smiled. "Sure."

"Don't be in the way," Gladys said.

She smirked. "Mom, when am I ever in the way?" As she followed Miranda into the small guest room, Stacie took in the sparse decor. Pictures of the coach during his football days were interspersed with more recent pictures. She recognized many of the players on the walls and smiled when she paused on a picture of Johnny poised to throw the ball.

"Ah, you've given your heart to a football player too, have you?"

Blushing, Stacie said, "Maybe."

Miranda laughed, her blue eyes sparkling. "Nice try, dearie. Now, where did I put it?"

"Put what?"

"Shawn's birthday present. It's his birthday, you know."

Stacie gaped at the woman before her. "No, I didn't know. Why didn't he tell us it's his birthday? Mom and I could have brought something."

Chuckling, Miranda said, "You already brought the best gift he could ask for. Your mother seems to be a perfect fit for my shy young man. And besides that, he doesn't like to draw attention to himself. But a mother never forgets when her baby was born."

"Is he your youngest?"

"Oh no, Shawn is the oldest of my children. But he's always been my baby, just as the others have. I'm sure if you asked your mother she would tell you the same thing. You might grow up, but you'll always be her baby."

"I suppose so."

"Poodle nuggets," Miranda said, stomping her foot. "Where did I put it?"

Stacie giggled. "What does it look like and I'll help you?"

"It's a red bag with white and black ribbons. I understand those are your school colors."

"Yep, though technically they're crimson and silver."

Miranda waved a hand. "Technicalities. I just can't seem to remember where I put it. I hope that boy hasn't been sneaking around in here."

Stacie spied the bag on the shelf of Miranda's closet. "Is that it, up there?"

~*~

Shawn didn't mind at all when his mother took Stacie to help her with whatever she was up to. "I hope you've had a good start to your month," he told Gladys as they cleared dishes from the table.

"It has been a great day," Gladys replied with a smile. "I had four parents call today interested in setting up tutoring sessions for their students. Thank you for suggesting business cards. I'm not sure I would have thought of them right away."

"You're welcome. I'm glad you're starting to see more success." He led Gladys to the living room and motioned for her to have a seat on the sofa. After stoking the flames crackling in the fireplace, he sat next to her. "Thanks for joining me tonight. It means a lot."

"Thanks for inviting us. I hadn't realized how homebound I was beginning to feel."

The glow in her sapphire eyes pulled him closer. He allowed his arm to drape around her shoulders, causing sparks to fire in his midsection. "You're welcome."

They sat in silence for a moment before Gladys frowned. "What are they doing back there?"

Shawn chuckled. "Don't know, but I also don't mind. It's nice to have some unobserved time with you."

Gladys smirked. "Why, Mr. Winston, that almost sounded scandalous."

"Oh come now, Mrs. Rosenthal, you can't tell me you never got involved with something a little scandalous. Not even once?"

She laughed. "Wouldn't you like to know?"

"Maybe I would."

"Tough luck, 'cause I'm not telling," she replied with an impish grin.

It was all Shawn could do not to let his jaw drop. This flirtatious side of Gladys was more alluring than anything he'd ever seen before. He brushed a wisp of hair from her face before returning his gaze to the fire. "You're a tease, Gladys."

She laughed and kissed his cheek, sending an electric pulse from the point her lips touched. "Sometimes," she admitted.

Shawn turned back to her. The firelight played across her elfin features and he wondered what it would be like to kiss her. Before he could talk himself out of it, Shawn lowered his lips to hers. His heart raced as warmth spread through him. "Sorry," he said, pulling back with a tiny smile. "I couldn't resist."

Blue eyes ablaze, she smiled. "Then don't resist." She pulled him back to her, their kiss deepening until a muffled giggle and cleared throat brought them back to reality.

"I'm so sorry to interrupt what is undoubtedly the best present you'll receive today," Miranda said, mischief lacing her tone. "But, I'd like a chance to wish you a happy birthday too."

Shawn glowered at her while Gladys turned to him with a frown. "It's your birthday?"

"Yes, but I didn't want you to feel obligated to bring something. Having you here was the best present I could ask for. Honestly."

"Well, hopefully this present will make a good second." Miranda handed him a gift bag in the Romance Valley High colors.

He opened the bag, pulling out layer after layer of tissue paper. "This is an awful lot of paper, Mom. Is that the present?" She smirked at him while he pulled out a statuette. In polished bronze, an ancient hunter stood with bow drawn. "Wow, Mom, this is great. But this looks like Dad's work. It's not possible..." his voice trailed away.

"David wanted to have it done for you for Christmas. But then he had that stroke," Miranda said quietly, tears coursing down her cheeks. She took a moment to regain her composure. "I'm sorry it took me so long to get it cast."

Shawn wrapped his mother in a tight hug. "It's perfectly on time, Mom. Thank you."

Chapter 14

Johnny set the rag down as his phone started singing.

SAVE ME!!!

He laughed. Stacie had texted him a few times since going to her dad's house the night before. *k. where r u?*

Portland. I'll give you the address, just get me out of here!

"Yeesh, no can do, Rosenthal." *sry, cant.*

What? Why not?

Johnny clicked his tongue. "Really, why do you think?" *2 far.*

Some Prince Charming you are.

u think im charming?
Not right now.

Laughing again, Johnny sent her a pouty face before continuing to wax his car. It was a nice day, for February, and he wanted to keep his baby looking her best. He saw Coach Winston running past. "Hey, Coach!" he called.

He jogged over. "Good morning, Johnny. A bit cold out for waxing your car, don't you think?"

"Nah, it's plenty warm." His pocket started to sing and Johnny pulled out his phone. He skimmed Stacie's message and laughed.

"What's so funny?"

"Apparently Stacie got herself into some trouble with her dad and she's begging for rescue. I doubt it's anything really serious because she would have told her mom if it was," he added when the coach looked ready to run to the girl's rescue and beat her dad. "If she wasn't all the way in Portland, I'd be happy to rescue her, but my mom would never let me drive that far on my own."

"Makes sense. By the way, next time you see Marco, you can tell him his little scheme worked. But I don't think Mrs. Rosenthal and I need any more help from you guys."

"What makes you think so?"

"Never you mind," Coach replied, color creeping up his neck. "Well, better finish that car of yours. See you Monday."

"Bye, Coach." Johnny chuckled and sent a text to Stacie updating her on this most recent chat with Coach Winston.

~*~

"Traitor," Stacie muttered as she got Johnny's poorly edited text.

"Sta-cie!" her stepmother called. "Would you come here, please?"

Rolling her eyes, Stacie got off the bed and wandered down the hall. "What do you want, Lyla?"

"I think you mean 'Mom,'" her father's voice called from the couch.

"Sorry, Mom."

Seemingly oblivious to Stacie's irritation, Lyla smiled. "I was thinking the two of us could go do some shopping. Just us girls. What do you say?"

Stacie wanted to tell her to go alone, but seeing her father scowl at her from the couch, she decided getting out of the house would probably do her some good. "Sure. Let me get my shoes and coat on."

With a bright smile, Lyla said, "I'll be in the car."

Stacie fought back a gag as she watched Lyla make a scene over her father. She went to her room and put on her coat and boots. Her phone buzzed.

will u survive?

"No thanks to you, Johnny." *Don't worry. I'm about to partake in some retail therapy. I'll be fine. See you Monday.* "I hope," she sighed. Forecasts were predicting a lot of snow, which might delay when she got home. She grabbed her purse and walked out to the driveway, where Lyla was waiting for her. The car was already warm when she got in and buckled her seatbelt. "Thanks, Lyla, er, Mom." Stacie about choked on the word. "I think shopping will be a lot of fun."

Lyla flipped her red hair over her shoulder as she turned to back up. "I thought so too. And I don't mind you calling me Lyla. I know you're never going to see me as a mom, and to be honest I'm okay with that. You're so close to my age it would be weird to have you call me 'Mom,' even if that's what your dad wants you to do. And I know you probably blame me for your parents' split. But I do hope that you and I can at least be friends. Maybe you can teach me how to do that super cool back flip you do at the football games."

"Maybe," Stacie conceded. She hated how easily Lyla had seen through her attempts to be polite.

"For today, let's forget about your dad and boys in general. Unless," she gave her a significant look, "you've got a young man you'd like to talk about."

Hoping the color in her cheeks wouldn't give her away, Stacie replied, "Not really."

Lyla giggled. "I thought there might just be a boy you were missing. But you don't have to talk about him if you don't want to. Today we can just be a pair of girls with unlimited credit and a nice car." She winked at Stacie as they drove further into the city.

Despite herself, Stacie enjoyed the time with Lyla. They giggled and talked in each of the stores, trying on far more clothes than either intended to purchase. After lunch, they went to a nail salon for pedicures. "Ah, this feels so good," Stacie sighed as the little jet tub started.

"It sure does. So, I did have an ulterior motive

for bringing you out with me. Nothing bad," Lyla added quickly when Stacie scowled. "But I have some news and I wanted you to be the very first one I told."

"Okay," Stacie said slowly.

Lyla took a deep breath, her expression nervous. "Stacie, how would you feel about being a big sister?"

Stacie blinked. "Are you serious?"

Lyla nodded, tears shimmering in her eyes. "You're unhappy, aren't you?"

As much as Stacie wanted to tell her yes, she knew it wouldn't be honest. The last few hours with Lyla had shown her to be kind-hearted and generous. She'd allowed herself to be vulnerable and admitted that the situation was awkward for her as well. While it didn't excuse the fact that she'd come between Gladys and Jesse, Stacie didn't really feel like she could totally blame the young woman her father had married. "No, I'm not unhappy. I'm just surprised, I guess. I never really thought about having any brothers or sisters. I've known for a long time Mom couldn't give me any."

"Your dad told me about her cancer. I'm so

sorry. That must have been scary for you as a child."

"It was," Stacie admitted, trying to push away the memories of her mother's ovarian cancer from her mind. "But you're going to be a mom. That's great."

"Really?" Lyla gave a hopeful smile.

Stacie grinned. "Really. Have you not told my dad yet?"

"No. I truly wanted you to be first. I know it will bring some changes into your life and I guess I thought I should do something to prepare you."

Laughing, Stacie said, "Not sure how prepared I'll be, but I think given the circumstances it's going to be a long time before I can teach you that back flip."

She giggled. "Yeah, probably best wait until after this little one makes an appearance."

"So when will the baby come? You don't look pregnant at all."

Lyla laughed. "It does take a while for a baby belly to show. But my doctor says the baby will come sometime in September. Hopefully it will be during one of your weekends with us. Then you can be right there to meet him or her."

"That would be awesome." And Stacie meant it. "Let's hope for a girl. A secret part of me always wished for a sister."

They continued their shopping with a trip to the maternity store to get a new wardrobe for Lyla and then to a baby boutique for some little items to start Baby's nursery. Stacie felt a special connection with Lyla. She'd shared something with her before anyone else. While she would never be a mother to Stacie, and both of them knew it, Stacie recognized that Lyla could be a great friend. She just wondered how her father would take the news.

Chapter 15

The next week passed in a blur as Gladys reveled in Shawn's attention. On Tuesday, he and his mother met them at El Torero for dinner and Thursday she invited them to come to her house for supper. Stacie had been unusually quiet since returning from her weekend visit to Jesse's house and Gladys couldn't help worrying that something had happened. When she expressed her concerns to Shawn, he shrugged. "I'm afraid I can't help there. I know she texted Johnny for rescue, but he seemed to think it was all in jest. The only person who could tell you if something went wrong is Stacie."

Saturday night she insisted on a girls' night. She

and Stacie dressed up and went out for a night on the town. They admired the multitude of hearts and strings of soft lights decorating the town square. Gladys watched her daughter and waited for an opening to talk about the weekend. It arrived when Stacie said during dinner, "I'm really glad Dad decided to take Lyla for a weekend getaway next weekend. I'll get to be home with you."

"I'm glad too. The house is always far too quiet when you're away." She paused and then said, "Stacie, did something happen last weekend? You've been very quiet about it, and frankly, it concerns me."

"No, nothing bad happened, Mom," Stacie said, though she frowned. "I just, I didn't want to hurt your feelings."

"How could you?" Gladys asked. "I saw all the shopping bags you came home with." She swallowed. "I think it's great that you and Lyla were able to have a good time together. You need to have a relationship with her."

"It's not the shopping and I'm not worried you'll be jealous. You've never really been the jealous type."

Gladys nearly laughed aloud. "Oh, sweetheart,

you have no idea."

Stacie looked at her plate for a long moment.

"Talk to me, Stacie. What's bothering you?"

"Lyla's going to have a baby," she blurted out.

Her heart twisting, Gladys said, "Ah. That's what you didn't want to tell me."

"I'm sorry, Mom, I just didn't know how to tell you. I mean, it's awkward enough because I'm not exactly a kid. I know how that works. And I'm sure it would be awkward for you, not to mention painful." Gladys looked up at her daughter. Seeing the concern in her eyes nearly broke her heart. "You never talk about it, but I assume you may have wanted more children than just me. You didn't get to and now…" Tears welled in Stacie's eyes. "I'm sorry, Mom, I just didn't want you to hurt any more than you already do."

Gladys smiled, though heartache for her daughter's worry and the children she longed for throbbed in her chest. "Stacie, honey, it is strange to think they're going to have a baby. But what a great opportunity for Lyla. I'm sure she'll be a wonderful mother and you'll be the best big sister ever." She took Stacie's hand. "Next time, just tell me. I was envisioning all sorts of terrible things that might have caused you to be so quiet."

"I will."

They continued their meal with laughter and when they returned home, Gladys wrapped her daughter in a tight hug. "I love you, Stacie."

"I love you too, Mom. Thanks for tonight. It was a lot of fun."

"Do you think poor Johnny survived two weekends without you?"

Stacie laughed and blushed. "Oh, I'm sure he was able to find something to occupy his time. I'm going to get ready for bed and finish up some homework."

"All right, sweetie. Good night."

"Good night."

Gladys watched Stacie go up the stairs before going to her own room. She'd ignored several texts during her evening with Stacie, but to finally get her daughter to open up was worth it. She skimmed through the texts and paused when she saw one from Shawn. *I tried calling but didn't get an answer. I guess you're busy with Stacie. Please call at your earliest convenience.* She dialed his number. When he answered she said, "Hi, Shawn, sorry I missed you earlier. Stacie and I decided to have a girls' night."

"Not a problem. I figured you were probably doing something with her. I, uh, I wanted to ask if you were planning on doing anything on Valentine's Day."

"Just eat my weight in chocolate and numb my mind with rom coms." When shocked silence filled the phone, she laughed, "I'm teasing again, Shawn. We've got to work on your sense of humor."

He gave a strangled laugh. "Sorry, I guess I'm not used to that yet. Do you really want to spend the day by yourself?"

"I suppose that depends on what you have in mind," Gladys replied.

"Well, I understand the Romance Valentine Charity Ball is going to benefit the hospital pediatric unit, and I figured that was probably a cause that's near and dear to your heart with how much time Stacie spent there. I thought we could go together, just a special date for the two of us."

"Oh, Shawn," Gladys began, touched that he'd remembered her talking about Stacie's childhood struggles, "I'd really love to, but what time does it start? Wednesdays are another of Stacie's volunteer days and I understand from Dr. Foster the puppies and mother are ready to come home."

Shawn laughed, though it sounded a bit nervous. "So she's convinced you to adopt all of them?"

She smiled. "I've yet to meet a person who can resist Stacie's pout. And since we don't have any allergies to worry about, I figured it would make up for the last thirteen years of saying no."

"Fair enough. Anyway, the ball starts at seven, but it looks to be kind of an open house type set-up, so I don't think being fashionably late would be a problem. Would you like to go? My mom would be happy to pick Stacie up from the animal shelter, if you think Stacie would be all right with waiting an extra day to bring her babies home. I'll even offer to help out."

"I'll talk to Stacie, but yes, I'd like to go with you. I always pick her up at five thirty. So perhaps if you would come help us on Wednesday, I'd be able to have a little extra time to get ready for our date. I don't know that I could convince her to leave the dogs there."

She could hear Shawn's smile. "I can agree to

that. Anything your new furbabies will need? Mom's been looking a bit down lately and I think a trip to the pet store would do her some good."

"Stacie's already bought a lot of the essentials, but if your mom needs an outing, a dog can never have enough collars and fancy tags."

"I'll tell her. See you then."

"Not Tuesday?" Gladys asked.

"I wouldn't miss tacos at El Torero," Shawn replied. "It's a pretty good tradition."

"That it is. I'll see you Tuesday then."

"Yeah." There was a pause before Shawn said, "I love you."

Warmth spread throughout her body as she replied with a smile. "I love you too."

~*~

Stacie covered up her squeal and went as quickly and quietly as she could to her room. She texted Johnny. *They just used the 'l' word!*

like?

No, love, you goose.

How do u know?

Scoffing, she typed, *I heard Mom say it. You've only got a few days until Valentine's Day, but you just might win. Maybe.*

I hope so.

She giggled. Johnny had to be feeling nervous with how close to the holiday they were getting. While she hoped he would win, just so she could go to prom with him, she couldn't quite see her mother moving that fast. Then again, she had just said "love" after only a couple weeks of dating. Stranger things had happened.

Chapter 16

Johnny took his seat next to Stacie in English class just before the bell rang. "Cutting it a little close, don't you think?" she asked him.

"Nah; besides, Miss Jordan loves me."

"You wish I did," the teacher teased as she walked past. She stood at the front of the class. "We're going to do something a little different today to celebrate Valentine's Day since you won't have school tomorrow."

"How many schools outside Romance do you think get out for Valentine's Day?" Johnny whispered.

"Zero," Stacie replied.

"Lucky us."

"I was lucky enough to find this on Facebook during the holiday season. It's a random question from author Janeen Ippolito. She does these every Friday, so those of you interested in pursuing a career in creative writing, I would encourage you to follow her page as these are great for character development or as writing prompts. So, the prompt is 'Secret Santa Time!' But for today, we're going to imagine a Secret Cupid for Valentine's Day. 'Your character(s)' or in our case, you, 'must give a present to their worst enemy. Who is it and what is the gift?' Discuss this in pairs and then I want you to write three to five paragraphs answering the question."

Johnny turned to Stacie. "So, you first."

"You know, a month ago I would have wanted to give my stepmother a new purse filled to the brim with moldy dog food. But, she and I have kind of reached an understanding, and in her condition that would probably make her puke."

"What condition?" Johnny asked.

"She's going to have a baby. So I wouldn't want to do that to her. Instead, we'll target the actual traitor."

"Traitor, really?"

"Yes. For Jesse…"

Johnny snorted. "Wait. Your dad's name is Jesse?"

"Yes, why is that funny?"

He started to laugh. "So Stacie's mom was Jesse's girl? Coach Winston is in love with Jesse's girl?"

Despite herself, Stacie felt a grin pull at her lips. "It's not funny."

"You're right, it's not funny. It's hilarious! So, what are you going to do to Jesse, other than help his girl fall in love with someone else?"

A wicked smile spread over Stacie's face. "I'm going to put a box of puppies on his bed."

"That doesn't sound too bad."

"I suppose not at first. But the puppies are bound to escape their box. Then the itching and wheezing will start. His eyes will water." She giggled. "He'll be miserable for days!"

Johnny blinked, unable to comprehend how the sweet cheerleader had transformed into such a malevolent creature. "That's just evil, Stacie."

"Maybe so, but he deserves it after what he put

my mother through."

"What about the puppies? They don't deserve to be abandoned like that."

Stacie smacked his arm. "I would never abandon puppies. After they've done their part, I'll take them home with me. Then Mom and I will never have to be lonely again."

"Your mom is well on her way to defeating her own loneliness, and if you were up for it," Johnny added, taking her hand in his, "I would be happy to make sure you aren't lonely either."

Blushing, Stacie said, "Really?"

"Really."

She smiled. "I'd like that."

~*~

On Valentine's Day, Shawn woke earlier than normal. He knew his mother wouldn't be up for a while yet, so he changed into running clothes and went out for his morning run. Nervous energy made him run longer and farther than he usually did. He'd talked to his mother about his plan and rather than quelling his nerves, the conversation had only multiplied them. What-if after what-if played through his mind like a never-ending horror story. He wasn't sure he'd survive until that evening. He stopped for a while to catch his breath, finding himself outside the Donaldson home where the Valentine's ball would be held. He could see decorations and teams of people setting things up. From the looks of it, the ball would have a very romantic atmosphere. That would be good. He was going to need it. He ran back home to shower and dress before running a few errands. First stop was Romantic Blooms to pick up the bouquets for the special women in his life. The flower shop looked like a garden had exploded, with dozens of vases of roses, lilies, carnations, and daisies filling every spare inch of room. Cheryl was filling a delivery truck when he arrived, and giving the driver specific instructions on delivery protocol. She saw him and smiled. "Hey, Coach. Here for your order?"

"Yes, ma'am."

She walked through the maze of flowers and carefully brought three arrangements over in a flat box. "You're getting to be quite a regular customer. May I assume your first bouquet was received happily?"

"I'd say so." Shawn smiled. "I hope you have a wonderful day."

"Well, it'll be busy, that's for sure," Cheryl replied. "Happy Valentine's Day!"

"And to you."

After stopping at Cicely's and then at the jeweler's, Shawn drove back home. He placed the bouquet for his mother on the little dining table along with a box of chocolates and a long thin box from the jeweler's. The other purchases he placed on the island in his kitchen. He was in the process of making omelets when Miranda entered the room. "Good morning."

"Good morning to you, dear." Her eyes fell on the table. "Is Gladys coming for breakfast?"

Shawn laughed. "No, silly, they're for you."

Miranda gave him a bright smile. "Shawn, you didn't have to do that."

"Dad would want you to remember that you're still a queen. Since I'm the only one around to remind you, I had to make it count."

Tears glistened in her eyes and she patted his cheek before examining the pink and white roses. "These are absolutely lovely." She opened the jewelry box and gasped as she pulled out a sparkling silver necklace with a ruby heart pendant. "Oh,

Shawn."

He kissed her cheek. "Happy Valentine's Day, Mom."

"I hope you've spoiled Gladys this thoroughly or she might get jealous," Miranda teased.

"Not yet, but I plan to tonight after we help them take their new puppies home."

~*~

As Shawn helped Cha-Cha into the carrier in the back of Gladys' car, he saw Stacie cuddling one of the pups. "Stacie, mind if I talk to you for a minute?"

"Sure, Coach." She handed the puppy to his mom. Gladys was still in the building, paying the adoption fees and filling out paperwork.

"Stacie, I'm sure you're aware that your mom and I have feelings for each other."

She grinned at him. "I'm pretty sure everyone is aware."

He gulped. "Well, yes. I would normally speak with her father about this, but as he isn't here and you'll be the most directly affected, I wanted to ask you. Stacie, I want to ask your mother to marry me."

Squealing, she threw her arms around his neck. "Really?"

"Yes, really," he chuckled, returning her hug. "Do I have your permission?"

Stacie attempted to look serious. "You promise not to break her heart?"

"To the best of my ability."

"And you'll be okay if I call you Dad?"

He swallowed down a lump of emotion. "I'd be honored."

She smiled. "Then you've got my permission and best wishes. Are you going to ask her tonight? Because I don't think I can keep this to myself for long."

"That is the plan."

"Good luck then, Dad."

Chapter 17

Gladys checked her reflection one more time.

"You look fabulous, Mom," Stacie insisted, a bright smile on her face.

"Thanks. You're sure you'll be all right? I don't know how late I'll be…"

Stacie rolled her eyes. "Mom, I'm sixteen. Besides, Johnny is taking me out to dinner tonight. So I won't exactly be starved for company."

Smiling at her daughter, Gladys said, "I suppose that is true." She stroked Stacie's cheek. "You've gotten so grown up."

"Mom, don't get all mushy. You'll mess up your mascara."

Gladys laughed. The doorbell rang. "Can you get that?"

"Sure."

While Stacie skipped from the room, Gladys looked once more at the mirror. The pink gown she'd found at Desiree's Dresses accentuated her curves while the ombré skirt swirled with each step. Without feeling too vain, she had to admit Stacie was right. She felt more beautiful than she had in months. She wrapped the warm capelet around her shoulders that had once belonged to her mother.

"Mom, your date is here!"

Gladys walked down the hall and into the entryway, where Shawn waited. Her heartbeat quickened as she looked him over. A dark red dress shirt complimented by a pink-and-white striped tie stretched across his broad shoulders. He held out a vase of red roses and a box of Cicely's candies. "Happy Valentine's Day, Gladys. Before we go, I do have something for Stacie as well."

"For me?" she repeated.

Shawn left and soon came back in with a smaller flower arrangement and box of chocolates and Johnny at his side. "I just happened to get here in time to see Coach trying to show me up," Johnny said with a teasing smile.

"You guys are spoiling me," Stacie said, taking the flowers Johnny was holding while Shawn set his gifts on the entryway table.

"Don't be out too late," Gladys said as the teens walked to the door.

"We won't be," Stacie promised. "Have fun!"

Gladys and Shawn watched them go before he asked, "Will you need a coat? It is cold out there."

"No, this will be plenty warm enough and won't wrinkle my dress."

He offered her his hand. She took it with a smile, enjoying the warmth and strength she felt. "Then let's be off. I'm interested to see what all they've done inside. I saw lots of coming and going this morning."

"I imagine you probably did," Gladys replied. She appreciated him holding her door as she got in and waiting until she'd pulled her skirt inside before closing it. When he got in the car, he leaned across and kissed her cheek. "You look beautiful, Gladys."

She blushed, grateful for the dark. "Thank you." Being with Shawn caused butterflies to dance in her stomach. She hadn't felt so nervous and giddy since she was a teenager. Soft, romantic music filled the short drive to the Donaldson House. Shawn once again opened her door and offered his hand as she got out of the car. They climbed the steps to the house, admiring the decorations and lights as they went inside. She drank in the sights and sounds of the ball. She'd always wanted to go, but Jesse had never been interested in it. Gladys smiled at Shawn after he took her capelet and hung it up next to his jacket. "They've made everything look so lovely."

"I see a refreshment table; can I get you anything?"

"A drink would be lovely."

They wandered through the rooms, admiring the decorations and talent of Romance's businesses. A room with romantic music playing and a tall replica of the Eiffel Tower caught her eye. "Oh, this is beautiful."

"It is."

"Hi," a woman in a green dress said. "I'm Phoebe Carmichael. Would you like some pictures taken?"

"Sure," Gladys replied. She turned to Shawn and wondered why he suddenly looked as though his tie was too tight.

"Great. Just stand in front of the Eiffel Tower right there. Yes, that's it. Um, sir, what are you doing?"

Gladys turned to see Shawn kneeling next to her. "Shawn?"

"I know I promised to take things slow, but I've never felt about anyone as deeply as I feel about you," he said, taking her hand in his. Her knees turned to jelly as the photographer began snapping photos and Shawn continued, "Gladys, if I promise to cherish you every day of my life and then some, would you do me the great honor of being my wife?"

For a moment she wasn't sure what to say. The logical side of her brain screamed that everything was going too fast. But in the soft glow of candles and Christmas lights with a starry, Parisian backdrop, her heart burst through the barriers she'd try to put around it. A smile curved her lips. "Yes, Shawn. Yes."

A small cheer went up from the couples in the room and Gladys blushed as Shawn stood and kissed her. "I don't have a ring for you, since I didn't want to guess the wrong size. Will this do for the meantime?" he asked, pulling from his pocket a long jewelry box.

She opened it to see a pair of intertwined hearts hanging from a golden chain. "It's perfect."

"May I?" He clasped the necklace and then placed his hands on her shoulders and pressed a gentle kiss to her cheek. "I love you so much."

Gladys smiled. "I love you."

Shawn handed the photographer his phone. "I know it's nothing like the nice camera you're using, but would you mind taking a picture for me? I know a few people who will be very anxious to hear how this went."

"Certainly," Phoebe replied. She snapped a few pictures and then handed the phone back to Shawn along with a business card. "If you need a wedding photographer, give me a call. Congratulations."

"Thank you."

As Shawn led her to the dance floor, Gladys felt her heart might burst. "I suppose we'll have to wait until the end of the school year?" he said.

"That would be wisest. Then we can continue to get to know one another," she replied.

"How many days until summer break?"

~*~

Stacie's phone buzzed and she pulled it from her purse. "Sorry," she told Johnny, "I normally wouldn't take out my phone during a date, but I'm waiting to hear back about something."

"That's okay," he replied. When she smiled broadly and put a hand to her mouth he asked, "What is it?"

She turned the phone around and he saw the picture of Coach Winston standing with her mother, a beautiful necklace sparkling around Gladys' neck with the caption *She said yes!* "Operation: Romance is officially a success."

"It's a shame I said they had to be engaged before Valentine's Day. I missed out by one day," Johnny said.

Nerves danced in her belly as Stacie smiled. "Well, if you think you could put up with me, I might still go to prom with you, if you asked."

His lips quirked in a grin. "Would you go to prom with me? Even though I lost the bet?"

"Yes, I would."

"The guys are going to kill me when they find out we lost by a mere twenty-four hours."

Stacie laughed. "I'll make the cheerleaders promise not to go too crazy with you guys."

"What about you? Are you really going to make me wear hot-pink lip gloss?" Johnny asked, making a face at her.

"You'll just have to wait and see, my dear Johnny," She smirked.

He groaned and Stacie giggled. She couldn't wait to write in her diary that night.

Acknowledgements

It's funny what goes into writing a book. Of course there are story ideas, fun characters, plot twists, and all the "craft" aspects of writing. But there are also fun little moments of serendipity which add flavor and zest to a great story. When I was writing *Katie's Chance for Romance*, I came to the sudden realization that Gladys Rosenthal really wasn't a bad person. She was a heartbroken woman desperately trying to feel young and important again after her husband left her for a "newer model." I wanted at some point to tell her story and help her find a happily ever after. When the idea of a shy, awkward football coach wriggled into my system along with some scheming teenagers at an unmentionable hour of the morning, I knew the cast was set. All I needed was for them to tell me the story. And what a fun time we had!

As many of you dear readers may know, real aspects of my life often creep into my writing. One of them was the writing prompt given by Stacie's English teacher. Janeen Ippolito is a real author I've been privileged to get to know through Facebook. She is also a writing coach and every Friday posts a random question for her characters. She invites other authors to participate and I've had a lot of fun delving into my character's personalities with those questions. The Secret Santa prompt is an actual post on Janeen's Facebook page and I did answer it with Johnny and Stacie. Readers who saw the post loved their exchange so much that, with Janeen's permission, I added her and the prompt to the story.

So thank you, Janeen, for your willingness to take a virtual visit to Romance. If you're interested in learning more about Janeen's work, visit her website at https://janeenippolito.com/.

I'd also like to give a big virtual hug to Kelsey Bryant for taking on the task of editing Operation: Romance on a tight schedule. I'm notorious for cutting things close to the edge and she was willing to work with me anyway! She did a wonderful job and I so appreciate it. Thank you! Those interested in editing services or in reading books by Kelsey can visit her website at https://kelseybryantauthor.weebly.com/.

And I could not do what I do without the love and support of my Prince Charming and our sweet children. I love and appreciate you more than words can express. Big hugs to my sweet Gary who gave Johnny his name. Mama loves you!

Miranda's Hot Cocoa

I'm one of those weird people who actually like winter. I love the snow, the quiet, and I don't even mind the cold. But most of all, I love being able to make hot chocolate all the time without anyone looking at me funny. Making it in a slow cooker is a nice way to have a steady supply available as well as allowing the flavors to really blend together. This recipe uses regular dairy milk, but if you have dairy allergies like two of my littles do, just replace the milk and chocolate milk mix with chocolate almond milk. They love it!

Miranda's Hot Cocoa

4 cups milk
8 T chocolate milk mix
1/2 cup dark chocolate chips
2 cinnamon sticks, broken in half

Mix ingredients in slow cooker. Turn on low for 3-4 hours, stirring occasionally. Serve with a cinnamon stick to stir.

Other Books in Romance

If you enjoyed reading about Gladys and Shawn, I hope you'll also enjoy these other Valentine's stories in Romance:

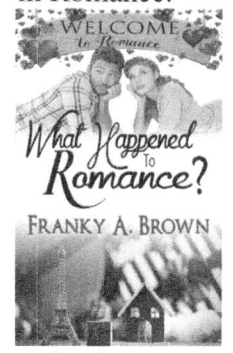

What Happened to Romance? by Franky A. Brown
For Mallory, romance is dead. It's up to Max to convince her it's alive and well.

Romantically Ever After by Liwen Y. Ho
Two best friends find romance in the most unexpected place: each other.

Fall Into Romance

Surround yourself in the romance of the autumn season with 10 heartwarming, sweet novellas from USA Today, national bestselling, and award-winning authors.

Each story takes you inside the heart of a small town—its people—and features adorable animal friends in need of a forever home.

Take a trip to Romance, Oregon, where falling in love has never been easier and happily-ever-after is guaranteed!

Finding Forever in Romance by Melanie D. Snitker

Brent's hands are so full he doesn't realize his heart is empty. But how can he convince Nicole to trust him and give them all a chance at the forever family they deserve?

Lost in Romance by Stacy Claflin

Work is Alisyn's life. Everything is perfect until the day her boss's son comes to town and takes her breath away. Will she risk it all for love?

At Second Glance by Raine English

Can an ornery French bulldog help a mismatched couple find love?

Blown Into Romance by Shanna Hatfield

Free spirit Brooke Roberts blows into Romance like

an autumn storm, unprepared to fall for the handsome rancher who gives her a reason to stay.

<u>Wired for Romance by Franky A. Brown</u>
Electrician Josh Chadwick can rewire his new client's house, but he can't do a thing about the electricity sparking between them.

<u>Restoring Romance by Tamie Dearen</u>
She's a big city chef who likes cats. He's a small town mayor who restores antiques. But even with feline allergies at play, true love is nothing to sneeze at.

<u>Finding Dori by J.J. DiBenedetto</u>
She's a loud, pushy New Yorker who drives him crazy. He almost ran her over with his truck. Of course they're perfect for each other…

<u>Katie's Chance for Romance by Jessica L. Elliott</u>
Five years ago she pushed him out of her life, but she couldn't force him from her heart.

<u>Chasing Romance by Liwen Y. Ho</u>
When pop sensation Chase Lockhart wants more than a room at Izzy Sutton's Bed and Breakfast, she must decide whether it's worth opening up her heart to him, especially when he's eleven years her junior.

<u>Lessons in Romance by Kit Morgan</u>
A rooster, a tortoise and love, oh my! Now if the humans could just figure out the love part, they might all live happily ever after.

If you've fallen in love with the quirky, fun, charming characters of Romance, be sure to watch for future stories. You can keep up on all the <u>Welcome to Romance</u> news on Facebook here: <u>https://www.facebook.com/welcometoromance/</u>

Other Books by Jessica L. Elliott

Other Sweet Romances:
Almost a Fairy Tale
Holly and Mr. Ivy
Scarlett and Blizzard
Katie's Chance for Romance
Of Snow and Mistletoe
Fantasies:
Charming Academy series
    Charming Academy
    Finding Prince Charming
    Prince Charming's Search
    Becoming Prince Charming
    The Ultimate Prince Charming
    Prince Charming's Quest
Talori and the Shark (illustrated short story)
Toil and Trouble
Coming Soon - Leticia's Song: A Charming Academy Short
Anthologies & Boxed Sets:
"Talori and the Shark" in Fantastic Creatures
"Leticia's Song" in Hall of Heroes
Katie's Chance for Romance in Fall Into Romance

Author's Note

Dear Reader, I hope you've enjoyed reading this book as much as I enjoyed writing it. In fact, I hope you enjoyed it more! Check out my website at the link below. There you will find links to my available books as well as links to my Facebook page and Goodreads profile. As you visit regularly you'll stay up to date on my works in progress, new releases and my life out here in small town Kansas.

If you have questions or comments about my books, you can email me or send me a postcard at the addresses provided. I love mail!

Wishing You Happily Ever After,
Jessica L. Elliott

www.JessicaLElliott.com

jessica@jessicalelliott.com

P.O. Box 584, Plains, KS 67869

Made in the USA
Coppell, TX
06 October 2021